Copyright Peter F Damsberg 2018

Also by the author;

Sterngard's Words

Silas Daniel Dyer

Stoies of Lost Souls

The Lazuli Series;

The Lazuli Stone

The Lazuli Brotherhood

THE ARCTURUS CODE

P. F. Damsberg

Prelude

Dag Paulsen Meldel had been named in the old fashioned way; his father's name was Paul, and so he took the paternal family name as his son with his middle name Paulsen. His sister had been so named. But Kristine refused to use her middle name Paulsdatter in either speech or documents. The closest she allowed herself to be to her paternal link was to call herself Kristine Paula if absolutely necessary. They both now had children of their own and, like most people these days, had left such nomenclature behind and chosen which names had taken their and their partners fancy at the time and broken the link with the old ways.

Dag was a police officer, a Detective Inspector. He was stationed at the Kristiansund police headquarters. Kristiansund that is, not Kristiansand, which was to the south of Norway; Kristiansund was on the west coast, a provincial town of some 24,000 people. But the jurisdiction of the police ranged further afield, over the Districts of Møre and Romsdal, an area of nearly 15,000 square kilometres and 280,000 people.

They'd had four murders last year, one or two more than usual. One was the girlfriend of an immigrant who's killed her during a domestic argument; the usual form of murder, another was of an elderly gentleman found dead on the road next to the airport and was still an open case and unsolved mystery. Another was an honour killing by an Afghan refugee, a quickly solved but politically delicate case. The final death was of a crew member on one of the Hurtigruten coastal ships that plied the waters along the coast of Norway still linking the isolated sea ports. Although there were, these days, almost as many tourists as there were local passengers now that air travel had taken over and roads and bridges improved. That was another case that had not been cleared up, but, as it was on board a ship had been handed over to National Criminal Investigation Service, Kripos, and Kristiansund could wipe their hands of it.

Dag was on duty when the call came in. The body of a man had been found. It was an out of the way place, a village on the coast; a settlement of scattered farmsteads and a few holiday cabins which were used by weekenders for the excellent fishing in nearby lakes. A policeman who lived halfway between Kristiansund and the village was on his way to secure the scene. Dag called for Martin Sorensen his Sergeant and partner in crime. They would both have to go to the crime scene. Forensics, there were at least two of them, were also told to make their way there but would no doubt take rather longer about it than Dag and Martin. Martin would have the blue lights on as soon as he got into the car.

It would be at least a two hour drive, part of which would mean taking the Seivika–Tømmervåg Ferry which would take about 25 minutes. It would give them a chance to have a coffee break and call the policeman to check whether he'd got to the scene and what he'd found.

1.

"No need for the lights." Dag told Martin as they settled into the car and put on their seat belts.

Marin gave a slight twist of his lips.

"We won't get across the ferry to Tømmervåg any quicker. Once we're on the open road afterwards you can open up; practice your rallying."

Martin face brightened a little.

"Ok boss."

They wove through what was light traffic in town; the rush hour was yet to start up, and even when it did the traffic in Kristiansund was never usually all that congested.

They took the road passed the airport where the previous body had been found. A plane was just taking off and reaching into the clear blue sky. It was spring, there was a chill in the air but the previous day's rain had cleared away. The sky sparkled as did the North Sea and the land. The trees and hills seemed to have taken on a high definition clarity.

"So, you reckon it's a local one?" Marin asked.

"Most murders, if murder it is, usually are. But that's jumping to conclusions, all we know for now is that it's a body; could be natural causes."

"Do you think they'd called us if it was?"

Dag glanced over at Martin. "No, the local doctor would have handled it."

"So, murder then?"

"An unexplained death, Martin."

Marin said no more but he knew that Dag thought it was a murder case; he had a nose for it.

They passed the airport and through the cutting that took the road to the ferry. As they approached they came behind a queue of lorries waiting to load.

Marin looked to Dag. Dag sighed and nodded. Martin turned on the blue lights and sped passed them. The ferry was just being loaded and they were waved passed several cars and on to the fore part of the deck. They would be first to unload.

As soon as they were parked Dag reached over to the back seat and took a thermos he always kept there; hot sweet black coffee. He got out and walked up a side ramp where there was a raised deck and he could watch the progress of the ferry as it ploughed through the open water of the Tromdheimsleia and then passed the almost bare and rocky islands before the larger island of Tustna and the road to their crime scene.

Ever since he was a boy he loved being on the water. He loved using the ferries, the movement of the water and even the smell of the dIesel. There were fewer of them now. New Roads had been laid and bridges built. You could get where you needed to go more quickly; but the romance of travel he remembered had been dIluted. And now they were talking of making the remaining ferries electric; odourless batteries powering the propellers removing the sense of smell and yet another link to his remembrances.

Martin stayed in the car reading a rally magazine.

As the ferry inched away from the quay Dag gulped down some coffee, screwed the cap back on the thermos and pulled his phone from his pocket. He called the office to get the number for the local policeman who might now have got to the scene and then called him. He was still on his way. As the call ended his phone rang. He looked at it. It was the chief.

"Yes Sir?"

He listened.

"All we know is that it's a body; maybe homicide, maybe not. There's a local on his way there now, he'll secure the scene."

He listened again.

"It's just a small village on the edge of our district. I don't think Trondheim will want to get involved, although they would be closer for forensics. Anyway it's probably a local matter; a domestic if anything."

The faint sound of the chief's voice crackled over the phone.

"I doubt it, Sir. Not many immigrants live out in the villages."

He paused. "Mind you, thinking about it, it's strange it was reported as a body. If it was a local affair whoever found it should have known who it was. They would have given a name, probably called the local doctor. They wouldn't have just said it was a body."

He paused again and listened to the chief.

"Well, there are some holiday cabins there; perhaps it's someone from one of them. It'll take us about another hour and a half to get there. Maybe less, Martin's driving. I'll call back as soon as I've got anything."

He pocketed his phone and watched the bow of the ferry slice through the water raising white foam. The grey of the sea now reflected the blue of the sky and the white foam mirrored the few white streaks of cloud that sailed high above him. He had another draught of hot coffee and, when he could see the arrival quay in the distance made his way back to the car.

Martin was still reading his magazine.

"The Chief's called." Dag informed him.

Martin rolled up his magazine and placed in the door compartment.

"Keeping an eye on us, boss?"

"Wants it to be over quickly and pleased it's unlikely to be anything political."

"Not likely to be immigrants, not out here."

"No, but as I told him, it's odd that no name was given. If it was a local they must have known who it was. So, someone else, maybe someone renting a holiday cabin. That'll mean a lot more work."

The ferry was edging towards the quayside the bow forward and being raised to allow the vehicles to drive off.

"I'll be there within the hour." Martin told him.

He turned the engine on as well as the lights and was off the ramp as soon as it had hit the ground.

The road only had light traffic. The lorries tendIng to bunch up and drive as a convoy when they left the ferry. The only thing to hold them up would be the inevitable farm tractors lumbering from field to field. The road followed a coastal strip of islands. Here the land was relatively flat with a regular scattering of farms with bright green spring fields. Between were evergreen woods and forests broken by outcrops of rock and peaty heath land. The winter winds from the North Sea stunted and bent the trees and shrubs to its will closest to the shoreline. It was a hard place to make a living from farming.

Now and then to their right would rise a large hill, some from low lying countries might call mountain, but not here.

Dag watched the scenery pass by. He tried his best to keep his eyes off the fast moving road and its corners and also away from electronic map on the dashboard that seemed to be Martin's pride and joy. He hated them. He believed in real maps, paper ones. He always carried a set on the back seat. A set covering their District at 1:50000 and a city map of Kristiansund. You knew where you were with paper maps. You could lay them out on a desk, pin them to a wall, set them on your lap; and you could read them, interpret them, and plan with them. You couldn't do that with those electronic gizmos.

The road wound around the outlines of the islands traversing from one to another over the new elegant bridges, sometimes almost turning back on itself before moving northward again. Martin was enjoying himself. It Didn't take much to imagine it as a rally route or, for that matter, a great ride on his Kawasaki Ninja ZX-6R. He decided to bring it this way the next chance he got.

A half hour into the journey Dag's phone rang. The local cop had got to the scene. Dag listened carefully.

"Very well. Just make sure that no-one gets anywhere near, and don't let anyone, even yourself, contaminate the scene. We shouldn't be more than another half hour or so."

Martin gave him a quick glance but then kept his eyes on the fast moving road.

"Not a local guy according to the person who found him – it's a him by the way. Lying on some undergrowth at the side of the village road not far from a farmhouse. Thinks it's someone who's renting a cabin opposite the farm."

"Any signs of cause of death?"

"He had the sense to keep clear but said that there was blood on the body's back just below the neckline. Very much like a gun-shot he reckoned."

"They all do a bit of hunting around here I bet, he should know what a gun-shot looks like."

"And I bet every farm's got a gun. As I said before, this looks like being more work than we might have thought."

"Maybe just an accident. Someone trips, gun goes off, shoots his partner and the other guy runs off scared."

"That would make our life easy. But life's not often easy. And I've just got a feeling about this one."

Martin knew his bosses feelings. And he knew that Dag was going to be right; this wasn't going to be straightforward.

It was coming up to 11 am when Martin slowed at a junction and turned left onto a side road. No more than a couple of hundred metres ahead was a car and police officer. He'd strung out some tape along the road to keep the scene clear. To the right was a wooded hill and to the left a farm – two large fields and, fifty meters ahead a farmhouse. Dag could just make out a cabin on the right amongst the trees standing just off the road a little further along from it. The cabin perhaps rented by the victim.

Dag and Martin parked their car a few meters from the tape. They strolled to the officer who gave Dag a perfunctory salute. He knew who Dag was; most officers within the Kristiansund force knew each other, by sight and reputation.

"So this is it?" Dag asked the officer.

The officer nodded. "No-one's been near, Sir, not whilst I've been here."

Dag pulled out two plastic cover from his pocket to cover his shoes together with a pair of gloves and pulled them on.

"Right, let's have a look."

He walked around the tape making a wide birth of where the body lay. He didn't want to disturb any of the ground around as much as possible and carefully scanned it to see if there were any show imprints around the body. There were none that he could see. Neither did it look like the body had been dragged of the road; the grass would have been flattened if that were so. The victim must have been shot where he stood. That in itself was odd. He would have been facing the tress with his back to the road, possibly standing still – it didn't look like he had been running from anyone – and he would have been shot where he stood, in the back. It made him think that the victim may have known his attacker. Perhaps he wasn't expecting any such attack and had been tricked into taking a few steps off the road to peer into the woods. It might, after all, be a shooting accident.

Dag knew straight away he had been shot. Even from this distance away the bloody wound was obvious.

He edged around the body. The man had dark hair, not long, nor closely cut. He wore trousers. Trousers, not jeans or hiking gear, or shooting wear, just plain ordinary trousers. Neither was his coat suitable for any of those activities; it was just a plain three quarter length coat. This was not someone out on a shooting trip or a hike. That put dent in Dag's idea of a shooting accident.

He approached the body and bent down to take a closer look. The face was unremarkable. He carefully checked the pockets trying not to disturb the body. He checked the coat and the trousers. Each pocket was empty. There was nothing in them. He looked at the man's hands. He had hoped to see a ring perhaps, but there was nothing. There was nothing on the body that Dag could see, to identify him.

He stood up and circled around the opposite side of the body taking out his phone and began taking some photos. When he was satisfied he stepped back onto the road. Now he had a smart phone, an uneasy acceptance of technology, he used it. Why wait for forensics to do everything. And who knew what changes might occur before they arrived. Best to get the freshest photos possible.

"Well," he said to Martin, "that wasn't much help; nothing on him at all."

"Hmm, odd. Everyone always has something on them."

"Not this one." Dag sighed. He now knew that his instincts were right.

"Who found him?" Dag asked the officer.

"The owner of the farm there." He said pointing. Adding, "That's the cabin he was renting." Pointing to the cabin Dag had noticed.

"Let's go and have a word." Dag said to Martin. "Stay on duty here," he told the officer, "I expect an ambulance and forensics will be here soon. Once they've done their job they'll take the body."

Dag and Martin strolled down to the farm.

By the time they reached the gate the owner was standing to the side of the building, between it and a large barn, waiting for them. To Dag the man looked a little nervous, but weren't people always so when the police came to visit. He was tall and slim and had dark curly hair. Hs had the look of someone who worked out of doors in both winter and summer. Dag and Martin passed through the open gate passed a tall silver birch tree that stood guard to the left.

"Morning." Dag greeted the man.

"Morning."

"And you are?"

"Eduard, Eduard Christiansen."

"You found the body?"

"Yes, early this morning, about 6 am. I was on my way up to Knut's, the farm just up the road." He said, pointing back the way Dag and Martin had come. "I was giving him a hand today."

"And did you hear anything last night. A guns shot perhaps, voices, shouting, anything like that?"

"No nothing."

"And anyone else in the house?"

"I'm here on my own at the moment, the wife's away visiting her sister in Trondheim."

"But you knew the man, you recognised him, knew who he was?"

"Didn't know him exactly. Of course I recognised him, he was renting the cabin." Eduard said point again, but this time towards the nearby building just of the road in the trees.

"Renting it from you? Is it yours?"

"Not mine, no, my nephew's. He was left it by an aunt, she lived there when she retired."

"So, how did the man rent it? On line?"

"On a web site I think, yes. My nephew would have seen to that."

"But you would have seen to gentleman when he arrived, given him keys, let him in?"

"Yes, I met him and sorted him out."

"And where is your nephew now? I suppose he must have the man's details?"

"He's working in Bergen. Worked at the gas plant, got promotion and they moved him there."

"We'll need your nephew's details. I imagine the man would have had a booking form, would have given you his details. You would have wanted to have checked that out before giving him the keys to the cabin?"

Eduard gave a slight cough. " I took him by his word. Who else would have turned up here to rent the cabin? He told me he'd agreed it all with my nephew."

Dag stared at Eduard for a moment. "How did he pay the rental?"

Eduard swallowed hard. Dag could see his large Adam's apple jump as he did so.

"It was a cash arrangement."

Dag gave a slight smile and a nod. "I think I get the picture. What was his name? How did he introduce himself?"

"He said his name was Petter, Petter Johansen." He paused. "But there was something odd about his accent. He spoke Norwegian well enough, but with an accent. Can't say I could be sure what it was."

"How long did he book it for?"

"Two weeks."

"And how long has he been here?"

This would have been the third day."

Dag stared at him for a moment longer. "Have you been over to the cabin today?"

"No, I've kept clear of it."

"You've got a spare set of keys I imagine, I didn't find any on the body."

"Um, yes I've got a spare set. I'll get them."

"Martin here will go with you, then he'll take a full written statement. I'd like us to get it all down whilst your memory is clear."

Martin went with Eduard into the farm house and within a minute was out again and threw the keys to Dag.

"Keep him busy until I've had a good look at the cabin." Dag told him. Then turned and walked back to the road and cabin. He looked down and felt a bit foolish. He'd taken off the gloves but hadn't removed the shoe covers. He shrugged; he would keep them on.

The drive left the road and turned to the left before reaching the door. It was not many steps before Dag, too, reached it. He took out his gloves and put them back on. He gently tried the door handle; pushed slightly and pulled. It didn't move, the door was locked.

'What.' He thought, 'had happened to the keys.'

He took the keys and unlocked it.

The door swung open, hesitated for a moment, smelling the air, then stepped in.

He always smelt the air. Eyes can deceive but you rarely found that your sense of smell fools or misleads you.

There was no real surprise. It smelled of a log cabin; the warmth of the wood and its polish, a slight dustiness, a hint of living and, of course, the lingering smell of coffee that seemed to permeate every Norwegian house. There was nothing untoward.

He stood in a small lounge area to the right of which opened into a small kitchen. Ahead to the left was a door left had been left slightly ajar. He could just make out the corner of a bed in what was the bedroom. Another door to the right was closed and he assumed it was the bathroom. It was a comfortable holiday place for one or two people.

The lounge was tidy. Nothing seemed out of place or even used. The cushions were neatly place on the brown leather sofa and he could not tell if anyone had recently sat there. There was no sign of any struggle.

He walked carefully to the kitchen area and scanned the surfaces. It was all clean and tidy. It looked as if someone had cleaned up ready to leave. He touched the kettle. There was water in it. Although clean there was a mug standing next to it and the only mark he could just make out when he bent slightly to let the sunlight catch, was a slight ring where a hot cup had previously stood.

Gradually he looked into each of the cupboards, both on the wall and below the work surface and sink. There were the usual cloths and cleaning materials and in the wall units more crockery and some coffee, sugar and a few cans of food. The fridge was bereft of any but one carton of milk unopened and out of date.

He walked back to the lounge and then to the bedroom door. He pushes it open with a single prod of a finger then walked in. Again the whole place appeared to have been tidied and cleaned. The bed looked hardly slept in. But it had bee. He could tell. It had been made but he could see that the pillows and duvet were not fresh, they had been used. If the man had slept here there was every chance that a small hair or some body fluid would give them a DNA sample.

There was a side table next to the bed with a single drawer. He opened it but found nothing inside. A white chest of drawers and a wardrobe were the only two other pieces of furniture. He looked through each draw and then the wardrobe. Again there was nothing other than some spare pillows and duvet in the wardrobe.

Where were the man's belongings? Where were his clothes, his luggage? He must have brought things with him. He'd not asked the farmer that question. And he hadn't asked him how the man had arrived. He clearly hadn't come in his own car or a hired one or it should be here. Unless, that is, his assailants had taken it with them. He would have to go back and ask some more questions if Martin had not thought of them, which he probably hadn't.

He took one last look around the bedroom and turned back into the lounge. There was a small wall unit with drawers which, again, he searched through, and again there was nothing. And there was a coffee table in front of the sofa. As he looked at it a bean of sunlight broke through the window and highlighted it. A part of it had been wiped, but not all. In a fine film of dust he could see three small marks. They looked like the small rubber feet at the bottom edge of a laptop. He took a closer look. He was sure that's what it was. At least he knew that whoever had been here had been using a computer. He wondered what the wifi signal was like here.

He left the cabin and locked the door behind him. Forensics would have to give this place a thorough going over.

Martin was just leaving the farmhouse when Dag got there.

"You got a full statement?

"Yes boss."

"Out of interest did you ask him how the man arrived here, did he have a car, and was he carrying any luggage?"

Martin smiled. ""Actually I did boss."

Dag raised an eyebrow. "And what did he say?"

"Came by taxi, a local guy, picked him on the main road at Stemshaug. Thinks he must have come by bus or been dropped off there. Carried a single backpack; canvas, green, rather old fashioned."

"Well done Martin. I wonder what happened to the backpack, no sign of it in the cabin. Find that taxi driver and get a statement off him."

"Was just on my way to do so, boss."

As they turned to leave the farmhouse they could hear the sound of vehicles back along the road towards the crime scene.

"Sounds like our friends at forensics have arrived already." Dag mused.

They walked back to the scene. They could see two vehicles, one from forensics and an ambulance car which would be ready to take the body to the morgue after their job was done.

As they neared Dag could tell there was something wrong. The local policeman, the two forensics team, and the ambulance driver were standing still facing Dag as if turned to stone.

The policeman moved a step closer. He looked white. Tried to open his mouth but nothing came out.

Dag gave a deep frown. "What the hell's the matter?"

Bjorn Hagen, the forensics team leader he knew well spoke.

"You seem to have lost your body."

Dag's frown remained. "Sorry?"

Bjorn nodded over the grass verge where the body was, or rather had been. It was not there.

Dag took a few steps towards the empty space his eyes widening.

"What the hell!?"

He turned and glared at the policeman.

"What the hell?" he repeated.

The officer swallowed hard. "They came Sir, and took it."

Dag took another step to stand face to face with him. "Who came. Who took it?"

An ambulance car Sir, the same as that one." he pointed. "They showed me ID. They said they were taking it away to the morgue."

Dag turned and glared at Bjorn. "Not yours I assume?"

Bjorn shook his head.

Dag turned to Martin. "Trondheim? Would they have got involved somehow?"

Martin shrugged. "Could have, but I'd doubt it. And they wouldn't have simply turned up and taken a body away like that."

"Check with them now." He thought for a second or two. "And then I want APB on all the roads. leading from here. I want that ambulance found. If you have to, get a chopper in the air. This should not be happening."

"Yes boss, right away." Martin agreed already pressing quick dial number.

Dag gave a deep sigh and turned to the others. "Well you may as well do whatever you can here and then I want you at the cabin down the road where the guy was staying. I want no stone left unturned – literally."

"And you," he said to the policeman. "You will tell Sergeant Sorensen everything you can recall about the people who picked up the body – I imagine it was more than one. Stand there and recall every last and tiniest detail."

"Now." He sighed again. "I need a walk. I need to think things through."

But his phone rang. It was the chief. He shook his head and gave another sigh.

"Martin," he said, "if the chief rings, apologise and tell him the signal's bad out here. I'll get back to him as soon as we've got something to tell him. But don't you dare tell him anything yourself."

"He's probably heard about the APB boss."

"Tel him you're just doing what I've ordered you to do. We're just chasing some possible suspects. I'm taking a stroll."

2.

Dag stared down the line of the settlement's road. It went straight before disappearing over the lip of a rise and then down to the coast. He knew it went to the shore line, he could see the blue water beyond and the opposite side of the 'sund', the stretch of sea, a bay, that encroached between the outstretched fingers of headlands.

He knew such a place well. The sight of it brought back the fleeting memories of when he was a boy. He remembered the freedom; the total lack of worries. The thought helped calm him. Down at the water's edge he was sure there would still be boats that the locals used to go out fishing, just as he did. In his grandfather's day fishing would have been as important, if not more, than farming. They would have relied on their catch to feed their families; they cured whatever was spare for the hard times, and sell what they might be able to. Now that cord of reliance was broken, these days it was just a hobby or an attraction for visitors.

He would take his walk down to the shoreline. He really did need to think, and calmly. Whatever was happening here was very much out of the ordinary. He didn't like it one bit. So far there was a complete lack of any evidence other than blood stains on the grass, an unknown victim with absolutely no identification, and now his body was missing; all within the space of a couple of hours or so. He really didn't want to talk to the chief.

He was already walking down the road as the thought were in his mind. To his left and further ahead to the right were a few more farm houses. As he approached the first he spotted a man near the gate. He would no doubt have heard what had happened and was hoping to get some juicy details. Eduard had probably already phoned his friends in the village and told them what was going on. You wouldn't be able to keep much a secret in as small a place as this.

Dag greeted the man. "Good morning."

The man looked at his watch, nodded and replied. "Good afternoon."

"So it is, time flies doesn't it. I was just wondering," He asked, "if you might have seen or heard anything last night that was out of the ordinary?"

"You mean the murder? No not a thing. Eduard phoned me up and told me this when he found the body; phoned the police first, of course."

"Of course, I'm sure he did." Although Dag wondered of that was so, maybe he wanted to get some advice first.

"And did you ever see this man, the one that's died? Did you know he was renting the cabin?"

"Eduard had mentioned he had someone renting it, yes. And I saw him a couple of times. Doing what you're doing, taking a walk down the road to the shore."

"Did you speak to him?"

"No I was working in the field. I gave him a wave but he didn't wave back. I'm sure he saw me, but he didn't wave back."

"I see. Did you notice how long he stayed out? How long it was before he returned; went back to the cabin."

"Maybe a couple of hours, no more, probably less, I don't spend my time looking at my watch."

Dag nodded and went to move off. "Oh," he added, "was he carrying anything when you saw him? A backpack maybe?"

The man though for a moment. "No I don't think he was carrying anything."

"OK, well, thanks for your help. If we need to we'll come and take a written statement."

Dag continued his walk. He would get Martin to take a statement and to visit the other farms here as well.

It was no more than ten minutes walk to get over the rise and down to the shoreline. There were five boat houses built around what was a small protect harbour. Three had been well looked after, in good repair and newly painted. The other two were old and unpainted, their weathered wood turned a light grey, almost white, by the salt sea. A final winter storm for the North Sea might finish them off. Five boats lay at anchor in the protected waters. Four were varying sized motor vessel, the fifth a more traditional wooden single-masted sailing boat. A final farmhouse stood out a field away on the most unprotected part of the shoreline.

He went to the water's edge and looked out over the calm blue bay across to the opposite shore. The sky was till clear and a light off shore breeze blue from the inland hills and mountains. He missed the summer days he visited his grandparents in such a place as this. He was content, happy and unworried but now, even though the few minutes of peace had calmed him, he felt the tightening of his stomach. He didn't have to think hard to know that this was not a usual case; not that any murder is usual or normal, but this, he already knew, was something very different.

He was about to turn and head back but there was a noise from the old boathouse that was close to his left. It sounded as if something had been knocked over. Was someone there watching him; maybe a fox holed up for the day.

He waited then turned as if to leave. Again a small sound, a scuffling of feet, he thought.

He turned to face the boathouse.

"I know you're in there. You may as well come out; show yourself. If you want to keep an eye on me you can do it face to face." He waited a moment. "Come on, out of there, I'm the police." He added, pulling out his ID and holding up to the invisible occupant.

There were footsteps from within and then the creaking of the old door as it opened wide enough to let someone out. From behind it came a small boy, about nine or ten Dag assumed.

Dag smiled at him. "It's me who's supposed to be spying on people, I'm the policeman."

The boy shrugged but stayed where he was beside the door.

"What's your name?"

"Aksel. Aksel Hansen."

"Where do you live?"

Aksel pointed to the nearby farm.

"Shouldn't you be at school?"

He nodded. "Wasn't feeling well."

"Ah, that old story. You look well enough now."

Aksel shrugged again. "You looking for the murderer?" he asked.

"You've heard about that have you?"

The screwed up his face. "Mum said at breakfast. Didn't fancy walking passed it to school"

Dag remembered seeing the school house just after they had turned into the village road, before they got to the body. "Well maybe that was a good idea."

The boy took a few steps towards Dag taking him passed the boathouse.

"Was it the man from the cabin?"

"Yes. Had you seen him? Maybe over the last few days?"

Aksel nodded. "Saw him yesterday; and the day before. He came down here."

"Down here? To the waterside?"

"Yes. Right there where you were standing."

"Did he do anything?"

"Just looked out like you did. But yesterday he threw something in the water and he left."

Dag stared at Aksel for a moment. "He threw something into the water? Something large or small, what did it look like?"

Aksel shrugged again. "Just small."

Dag looked out into the water. "How far would you say he threw it?"

Aksel came up to his side. "Not far." He said, pointing. "About there."

Dag judged it to be no more than five meters."

"Is it deep there?"

"Not very. As tall as me."

"Well, thank you Aksel, that's been very useful."

Dag looked over to where the boats were moored. "Do you know who owns the boats? Maybe they'd let me borrow one?"

"Don't expect there's anyone around to ask. One's my dad's but he's gone to Trondheim. There's an old one in the boathouse. You can use that, it was my granddads but its mine now really, he left it to me."

"Come on." Aksel added, turning to the boathouse and holding out his hand for Dag to take and follow him.

"Are you sure?"

"You're a policeman, you can take it; I've seen it on TV."

"You mean requisition it. Yes I suppose I can."

Dag helped Aksel swing the boathouse door fully open. In it was an old rowing boat. Dag walked around it. "Will it float?" He asked dubiously.

"Aksel gave his usual shrug. We've only got to go just out there?" He pointed,

"We?" said Dag with a raised eyebrow.

"It's my boat." Aksel said with certainty.

"Hmm, well, you can help with the oars I suppose." It did at least have oars as Dag could see. "Come on then, let's get it out."

It was easier than he thought. It rolled smoothly over the well worn lags that made up the short slip to the water. He imagined that Aksel spent some taking what care of her that he could perhaps remembering the days that his grandfather had taken him out in it fishing.

It was into the water and they jumped in. Aksel knew what he was doing and only had to make a couple of strokes to get them to the spot he'd pointed to. He brought in the oars and peered over the side. Dag joined him.

Aksel had sharp eyes. "There!" he exclaimed, pointing into the water and at something caught between tow rocks.

Dag looked hard. It was a small package; plastic with something in it."

"Have you got a net or something we can use to get it out?"

"I'll get it!"

And before Dag could utter a word Aksel was over the side, fully clothed and into the water."

"Aksel!" he shouted reaching out too late to stop him.

It only took Aksel a moment. He had reached down and pulled to item from between the rocks and popped up holding the side of the boat, holding it up, with a big smile on his face.

"Dag grabbed him. "Aksel! What the hell do you think you're doing, the waters freezing and you've got all your clothes on!"

He pulled and dragged Aksel aboard.

Aksel just smiled and was breathing heavily; the cold water had taken his breath away. But he held up the small plastic packet for Dag.

"Your mother's going to kill you!"

"She's out at work." Aksel managed to say.

Dag took the packet from him. "Come on, we'd best get you back as quickly as possible. You need to get back home, get warm and change into something dry."

Dag took the oars and rowed the few meters back. They quickly pulled the boat back in and Dag escorted him across the open field and back to his farmhouse.

"Right, you get inside and get dry and changed. Get yourself a hot drink as well. I'll come back later and check on you. But not a word to your mother or anyone else, not till I get back, do you understand?"

Aksel nodded. He was only too pleased for his mother not to know.

"Thank you." Dag said to him with sincerity. "Thank you very much for this. You've been a very special help to me, I won't forget it." He smiled and ruffled Aksel's hair. "Now, get inside."

Dag took a good look at the package. A sealed plastic bag. He could see what was inside. In it was a memory stick and a few coins. The coins probably used to give it some weight so that it would sink.

Dag closed his hand around it then put it in his pocket. It was time he got back to the crime scene and to find out what forensics and Martin had been up to.

3.

When Dag reached the cabin Bjorn and his compatriot were there with their investigation of it under way. There clearly hadn't been much they could do at the murder scene.

"Anything from the scene?" Dag asked Bjorn.

Bjorn just gave him a look. "We'll get some DNA from the samples, I'm sure; but without a body ..."

Dag took his phone out. "I've got some pictures on my phone, they might help."

Bjorn's face brightened. "You thought to do that? Good."

"I'll send them to you; email?"

"Yes, you should have my email address?"

"I'll send them now."

Dag fingered his phone. He didn't thumb it like most others seemed to. He couldn't get the hang of using his thumbs on the small version on the phone's keyboard, he was too used to using a keyboard the old fashioned way. There was a beep as the email was sent.

Martin came towards him from the where the body had lain.

"What's new?" Dag asked him.

"The Chief's been on again. He's getting quite annoyed."

"He's always annoyed, he enjoys being annoyed. Hates not knowing what's going on. Wouldn't be surprised if the press has already got to hear of it and they're eon his back wanting a statement. Anything else?"

"The roads are being checked. Both ends; towards Kristiansund and Trondheim. Trondheim are helping out."

"That's good of them."

"And I called in a favour. Friend of mine's one of the pilots on the police helicopter. They had a training flight planned and he's agreed to use it to check out the main road as much of the route between Kristiansund and Trondheim as he can."

Dag brightened. "Well done. Let's hope we get something from that. Whoever it was couldn't travel too far and not as fast or far as the chopper can get."

"And I had a word with the farmer up the road, at the junction."

"Anything?"

"Didn't hear or see anything last night, no. But he did remember something else. Two or three weeks back, he wasn't sure; A black car parked early one morning outside the school house. He'd only just got up. Beside it there was a man, he was talking to Eduard's nephew," he looked at his notes, "Johan Christiansen's his name by the way. They didn't talk for long and the car turned round and drove off. He just thought it was a bit odd."

Dag nodded slowly. "Hmm, could mean something. Anything else?"

"The taxi driver phoned me back. Remembered that, when he picked up our man, there was a dark car parked further up the road next to the local church. Could have been someone who dropped the guy off."

"No better description than that I suppose."

"Afraid not. Oh, and I tried that nephew's phone number, it was turned off or not working. The office is asking Bergen to check out his last address."

"All points to something odd going on though doesn't it."

"What else of interest is around here?"

"There's a village a couple of K down the road, it's got a shop and post office. There's a large fish farm there, salmon, fry, they bring them on from eggs and then sell them on to the larger farms to grow full size. And there's a chemical plan along the coast from it. A fair size. Produces methanol so it says on its web site, from gas that gets pumped ashore. The hot water it produces goes to the salmon farm. It's where Eduard's nephew worked"

"Well let's take a run out to that village. If there's anyone who knows what's going on around here it'll be the shopkeeper and post master."

When they got back into the car Dag immediately reached for his thermos. He poured a cup of coffee. He grimaced. It was just luke warm. He drank it anyway but he needed fresh and hot.

"And you boss? Have a good stroll?"

"I thought it would clear my mind. It did, to begin with. Then I ended up with more questions than answers. But interesting ones."

He said no more and Martin revved the engine and headed for their destination.

They drove into the shop car park. There were several other cars and a couple of 4x4's parked there. It was a fair sized supermarket for its location. Beyond it Dag had noticed a couple of timber yards either side of the road that led out beyond it. Martin parked up and they went into the shop.

Dag showed his ID to the woman who was on the till and asked if they could talk to the manager. She pointed over to another woman at a counter that acted as the post office.

"Good afternoon. Detective Inspector Meldel, this is Sergeant Sorensen. Can we have a few words."

"Oh, yes, certainly." She said keenly. "It's about that murder I expect?"

"Word gets around." Said Dag.

"Shall I come round?"

"If you wouldn't mind. Is there somewhere we can talk?"

"I've got an office just back here, we can go there."

They followed her into a small office with one desk and two chairs. She automatically took the office chair in front of the computer and Dag took the other leaving Martin standing.

"We were just wondering if you had seen any strangers over the last few days." Dag asked her.

"You mean did I see the man in question? Well, I think I did. It must have been him, we don't get that many visitors here, not at this time of year. Later in the summer and school holidays there's more people about. Fairly tall, dark hair, carried a backpack. He came in the day before yesterday, in the afternoon, about this time. I don't think he drove here, probably walked."

"Can you remember what he bought? I expect you still have the till receipt for the day."

"Oh, I won't have to look at that, I can remember."

'I bet you do.' Thought Dag.

"He bought some milk, bread and cheese, some apples, a few bars of chocolate and coffee."

"Not much of a meal. How did he pay?"

"Cash." She replied. "Oh, and he bought a stamp. One for a letter to England. He had the envelope with him. He put the stamp on and gave it to me for posting. A brown envelop, it was, about this size." She showed him a wide narrow envelope suitable for A4 paper.

"A letter for England he said."

"London, England. I noticed that. The England was underlined and London in capital letters. But that's all I saw. I didn't really take that much notice, it just caught my eye that's all."

"Hmm, well that's useful, thank you very much."

"Do you have CCTV?" Martin asked her.

"Yes, we do, even out here you can't be too careful. We've got to have it for insurance anyway as we're a post office."

"Perhaps you'd be kind enough to let us have a copy of the recording."

"Oh, of course. It's just here. It's on a disc. She reached over to a drawer and pulled out a disc, first checking the date that was on it. "Here it is."

She handed it to Martin.

"You don't do coffee do you?" Dag asked her. He was holding his thermos that he'd brought with him. "Mine's gone cold, it's been a long morning."

She smiled. "I'll get some made up for you." She looked at Martin. "Anything for you?"

"I'll get something from the shop. And something to eat, I'm staring. Do you do sandwiches?"

"In a cool cabinet. I make them myself."

"Get some for me as well, Martin." Dag instructed him. "I can't see us getting a hot meal for a while."

They left the shop with sandwiches and hot coffee. Dag took a cursory look around.

"You said there was a chemical just along the coast?"

"Yes, not far in a straight line, but about three and a half k by road. It's where that nephew worked before he got promotion."

"Let's go take a look at it."

The road started out back to the village but half way they took a right turn along a well made access road which curved around a low hill covered with stunted fir trees and patches of open ground. It came to a halt before a gate and guard house. They parked outside and went to the window.

It slid open before they reached it. Dag was already pulling out his ID and bringing up to the face of the man that peered through at them.

"D.I. Meldel and Sergeant Sorensen. Can we have a quick word?"

"Certainly, I'll come out. It'll be about that murder will it?"

"Just a few questions of my own Sir."

The man was quickly out and standing before them clearing his throat.

""Everyone seems to have heard about the murder. Obvious in a small place like this. Have you seen any strangers around here recently?"

"Thought you might ask that. Two days ago. Bet it was your man. He was out walking. Came up the road towards here but stopped some distance back. Stared at the place for a while. I came out to get a better look at him but he was quite far off, by the turn in the road there. Then he turned and walked off. But not down the road. He set off across the land. There's an old track that goes across it and over the hill; takes you all the way back to the village. That's where he was going I expect. Fancied a walk on the wild side."

Dag and Martin looked back along the road.

"And you never saw him again?" Dag asked the guard.

"No that's the only time. The next thing we hear someone's dead. Him I expect?" He looked questioningly at Dag.

"Dag smiled. "You've been a great help, thank you very much. If we need a written statement Sergeant Sorensen here will be back."

They turned and went back to the car.

"Let's take a look up there where he saw our man." Dag said.

Martin drove just beyond the curve of the road where the car would not be spotted by the guard and they walked back to the spot that had been pointed out.

A short walk along and they could see the track that led off the road and out into the trees.

"Have you got a map on your phone?" Dag asked Martin.

"Martin took out his phone. "On here, yes."

"Now the time's to use it and get a bit of exercise. Follow the track back to the village. See what you can see. You won't get lost will you?"

"Hike across there? Now?"

"Yes now Martin. All you want to do is spend your time behind a car steering wheel. You need some exercise, it'll be good for you. Retrace that man's steps. Take a good look around. I'll drive back to the village. I'll see you there when you return."

Martin's shoulders sagged. He looked miserably at his phone. "What if I run out of power?"

"Instincts, Martin , use your instincts." He called out as he got into the car.

Martin watched Dag drive off, muttered some swearwords and set off along the track.

When Dag reached the cabin his phone rang. He knew that this time he must answer it.

After Dag explained as much as he wanted he listened to a long one sided conversation. He hadn't told the Chief too much, after all, what he knew so far was not specifically evidence, not yet at any rate, it was just a tangle of spurious information. The Chief wanted details, evidence. And Dag decided that that was in short supply so far. And anyway, the less the Chief knew at this stage the less he might be tempted to pass on to the press. Dag didn't think they needed lots of juicy snippets of information to start them speculating. He had no doubt that the press would be on their way there now anyway, in fact he was surprised they weren't already there. He sat in the car for a moment and drank two cups of dark strong coffee, and gobbled down the sandwich he'd got from the shop.

Bjorn came out of the cabin as Dag got out of the car.

"Chief on your back?"

"When isn't he?" Got anything useful?"

"You saw the place yourself, almost as clean as a whistle. Either the occupant or someone else did a pretty good and quick job of cleaning up. But we did find the bullet at the murder scene; a .22, not a large round but at close range very effective. A 9mm will go straight through a man, a .22 can ricochet about a bit inside before exiting, can be quite nasty. It had gone right through the man and was embedded in the ground. So we'll able to match to the type of weapon, probably one small enough to be concealed easily, and have the marks that can match it to a specific weapon if ever you find one."

"We're taking as many swabs and samples as we can. With a bit of luck there will be some DNA traces, especially on that coffee mug and within the bed clothes."

"You'll be off back to Kristiansund soon then?"

"Yes, not more to do here. And you?"

"Think we'll hang around here. There're more things to find out, I'm sure; and we're not going to find out anything anywhere else, not for the time being at any rate. I'll find out if there's anywhere to stay for the night, one of those other cabins maybe."

"We'll get a report to you as quickly as we can but it'll take a few days."

Dag nodded. "Think I'll go and talk to that farmer again, see what accommodation we can get."

Dag set went over the road and knocked on the door. He explained what he wanted and Eduard sent him off to the next farm and the other farmer he'd spoken to earlier. He was the owner of two of the other cabins further down the road. As far as he knew there were no other people staying at either of them at the moment.

It didn't take Dag long to arrange one of the cabins for the night. The farmer would have preferred cash, of course, rather than have to make up an invoice for the police department and then wait for goodness knows how long before getting paid. But he seemed satisfied enough. He'd probably upped the rate knowing he'd get paid regardless. He also offered to arrange a hot evening meal for Dag and Martin, cooked by his wife. Dag thanked him. The thought of it brought back in his mind the smells of his grandmother's farmhouse cooking and made his stomach grumble despite just having eaten the sandwich.

The farmer gave him the keys and he took a quick look around the cabin. There was one bed in the bedroom, that was his, and a sofa bed in the lounge area, that would be Martins.

Satisfied, he went back to the crime scene cabin. Bjorn and his partner were getting ready to leave; the ambulance car had long since gone, with no body to pick up. As they were about to set off Martin came through a track in the trees and onto the road just a matter of meters towards the schoolhouse.

"These shoes aren't the thing to wear for trekking across the countryside." He complained.

Dag looked down at them. "No, I suppose not. You look a bit puffed, you should get more exercise."

Martin just gave him a silent stare.

"So," asked Dag, "anything of interest."

"This." said Martin, as he held up a sandwich wrapper delicately by thumb and forefinger.

Dag waved to Bjorn who was just about to drive off. Bjorn turned the engine off and they went over to him. Bjorn produced an evidence bag and carefully took the wrapper from Martin.

"That should be all for now." Dag told him. "I'll look forward to your report."

Turning to Martin he said. "We're going to stay here tonight; I can't see the point of going all the way back to Kristiansund. There's a bit more digging around I'd like to do. I've got us one of the other cabins up the road there."

Martin sighed. "We haven't even got a change of clothes."

"You can have a shower and spruce yourself up. The owners provided what we need. And he's arranging a hot meal for tonight."

"Well that's something I suppose."

"Where abouts did you find the wrapper?"

"Ah, yes, interesting. The track leads up a hill. At the top it overlooks the chemical plant. That's where the wrapper was. Our man must have stopped for a break there."

"And taken a good look at the plant?"

"You can certainly see everything that's going on, yes. Spying on it, I don't know; could have been."

"Hmm, another visit there tomorrow I think."

"Anything on our mystery ambulance vehicle?"

"Nothing. The chopper had to return to base. My mate gave me a call. They saw nothing. No reports from the ground either."

Dag nodded slowly. "Somehow I thought not."

"The Chief?" asked Martin.

"Yes, he's called again, and yes I've spoken to him. Or should I say he spoke to me. But I kept things pretty close to our chest for now. After all we've got no reel leads or evidence yet have we?"

They both looked around as they heard the sound of vehicles coming along the main road towards the village.

"Uh oh, looks like the press." Mused Martin.

"Come on; let's get away from here and to our cabin. Tell the officer," who was still standing guard at the murder site now covers with a plastic sheet, "to keep them well away from it, and tell them nothing except that they'll have a statement tomorrow. And you better make a call and see if we can get him a replacement for a night shift."

They had both showered and made themselves comfortable when the farmer brought a meal over to them. Dag thanked him and at the same time suggested that he tell the press as little as possible, and certainly not to let them know that he was staying in the cabin.

The aroma of the cooking when they lifted the pot's lid again reminded him of those days as a boy. Fishballs, potatoes, some swede and a bowl of crisp bacon fried in butter. It was the best meal either could remember having in a long time.

"Now, those are the best fishballs I've had since I was a kid. Exactly like my grandmother used to make."

Martin could only nod happily and agree.

"Have you got your laptop?" Dag asked.

"Yes, here," said Martin.

"I want you to have a look at something."

Dag took the small plastic package containing the memory stick from his pocket.

Martin stared at it frowning. "Where did you get that?"

"Not at the crime scene or cabin. I found it somewhere else, so not, as yet, evidence. I'd just like to know what's on it. If it looks like it relates to the case, then we'll make it official."

Martin gave him a dubious look. "Ok, let's have a look."

He plugged it in to his laptop and waited a moment, then clicked to open up the device.

"Hmm. I can see there's a file on the directory, but it's not a type I recognise and not one that will open automatically with any software I've got. The suffix is .ATS. I'll take a look on line and see if there's any software that'll open it."

Martin clicked away for a moment. "No, nothing. According to the internet there's no such suffix. Whatever it is there's no way of me opening it;

you'd need some experts to have a go. I'd guess it's encrypted." He paused. "So where did you find it?"

"I'll show you tomorrow. But for now I think I'll get some rest."

4.

He lay down to sleep, but he didn't rest. His mind went through all that had happened and what they'd found out during the day. He ran through each detail from beginning to end. From the start and then all over again making sure he remembered everything and leaving nothing out.

There was only one conclusion that he could come to. As he had felt from the start, this was not a normal murder case; if any murder was in any way usual. There was something much more mysterious and interesting about this one. It went; he both knew and felt, beyond what would be his normal remit for an investigation. It was only too clear to him that, as soon as the Chief had more details, the case would be passed on as quickly as his boss could do so into the laps of national investigators. Whatever and whoever was behind this murder went beyond the confines of their District. But he didn't want to give up on it yet. He wanted to get his teeth into and stay on the case for as long as possible.

Firstly, tomorrow they would go back to the chemical plant. Secondly, he wanted the Bergen police to find Johan Christiansen, the cabin's owner. It was essential they got their hands on his computer. It may be the only link and data they had to the murdered man; that is, if he had made contact with Johan through the internet.

And Johan's promotion and leaving had been fortuitous for whoever was behind this. Was it coincidental or was his meeting two or three weeks earlier linked to the hire of the cabin?

The next morning they set off early. Two officers were now at the crime scene, the night shift along with the local who had returned early. Two cars were parked close to the school house. It was clearly still early for the reporters who were still snoozing inside them. Martin sped passed before they could rouse themselves and follow them.

The gate to the plant was busy with workers arriving for the morning shift. Dag and Martin parked a short distance from it and waited for the queue to die down. When it had they drove up to the gate. The same guard was on duty as the day before.

"Oh." said the guard. "You're back again already. Do you want to take my statement?"

"Actually," Dag told him, "I'd like to see whoever manages this place."

"Um, well, the only one in this morning is the duty manager."

"And he is?"

"Kevin Vikan."

"Then perhaps you can tell him we'd like to see him?"

"Yes, of course, I'll give him a call."

He went inside his guard hut and made the telephone call. His head peeked out in just a minute. "He says you can go in. If you drive over to that building," he pointed it out, "he'll meet you at the door."

He came out, lifted the barrier and they went through. By the time they parked at the offices door Kevin was waiting for them.

He introduced himself, asked them in and took them to a small room adjacent to the reception area. There was just a table and three chairs and was probably used as an interview room; which was appropriate for that was what this was, although in reverse to the usual ones.

"Don't tell me," Kevin opened the conversation, "this is something to do with that murder."

"We're just making general enquiries throughout the whole area before we head back to Kristiansund. I just wondered if there had been anything unusual happening in the last few weeks, anything out of the ordinary, not the usual routine; unusual visitors, any strangers seen in the area. Perhaps a member of staff may have reported something, or maybe something you noticed yourself?"

Kevin pursed his lip. "No nothing, nothing at all. I've not noticed anything and no-one's said anything to me. I'm not the only manager though; perhaps one of the others? Or Mr Jørgensen, he's the overall manager. But he's not in today, in fact he's on annual leave, went yesterday. He'll be away for two weeks."

"It was just that the guard mentioned something to us yesterday. He saw a hiker now far from the gate a few days ago, could have been our victim. Did he say anything or report it as far as you're aware?"

"Not as far as I know, no. Unless someone actually tried to enter the place he'd have no need to."

"Oh well, if there's nothing you can think of we'll be on our way. But if you do remember anything, anything at all, no matter how small a detail let us know; Martin here will give you our number. And if you could ask the staff the same questions I'd be grateful."

Kevin nodded as Martin handed him a card with their contact details.

"If I hear anything I'll get in touch."

They all rose and exited the room. In the reception area Dag stopped suddenly.

"Oh," he said, "there was one other thing."

"Yes?" frowned Kevin.

"Johan Christiansen, he worked here."

"He did up until a couple weeks ago, yes."

"Do you know what date he left?"

Kevin thought about it. "I'm sure it was the 23rd."

"So," Dag calculated, "sixteen days ago. I heard he got a promotion and moved to …. was it Bergen or Stavanger?"

"Promotion? He may have got a better job somewhere else I suppose, but he didn't get promotion with us. A good enough worker and all that, and a nice quiet guy, but no, he just handed in his notice and left, didn't even give a week's notice. Put us out a bit, someone had to cover his shifts and it's not easy to get replacements around here."

"I see, well thanks for all your help."

They got back into the car and drove to the gate. The guard came out to raise it but Dag got out to talk to him.

"Just another quick word if I may." He said pointing to the guard house.

He followed the guard in.

"You have a visitor's book I imagine?"

"Yes, well two really, one's for visitors the other for the tankers and regular trucks that come in and out. The workers don't have to sign in of course they've got passes."

"The visitors book, if I may?"

"Of course, here it is."

Dag flicked through the recent pages, there weren't that many visitors.

"If you don't mind I'll just take a copy of the pages with my phone. It'll save me having to take it away as evidence. You'd much prefer that I expect?"

"Oh, well, yes I suppose so."

"Thanks." Dag took out his phone and copy the few pages that showed the visitors coming and going over the past few weeks. "Well that'll be all for now and hopefully we won't have to be back."

He went back to the car. The guard followed him to open the gate. Martin was in the driving seat but Dag asked him to move over, he wanted to drive. He was about to get in, stopped, and asked the guard one more question.

"You book every visitor in and out don't you? No exceptions?"

"Of course, nobody enters without booking in."

Dag gave him a silent stare then said. "But you didn't book us in did you?"

The man blinked several times his mouth opening and closing again before he spoke. "Well, you're the police aren't you, you showed me your ID."

Dag nodded slowly. "Yes, we're the police aren't we?" Then he got into the car and drove through the gate.

"There're a few things you can be doing on that smart phone of yours." Dag told Martin as Martin plugged it into the dashboard to recharge. "Firstly find out if there's been any more news from Bergen. And tell the office to do a check on airline manifests; anything leaving Kristiansund or Bergen on the or during the week after the 23rd, see if Johan Christiansen's name turns up. Maybe add Stavanger to that as well. Also, who do we have back at base that you'd call a computer whizz, I'd like someone to have a look at that memory stick before it's bagged up as evidence."

"I'll get onto it." Martin replied as he began to dial.

Dag lost himself in thought whilst he drove back to the village, not listening to Martin's conversations, allowing them to merge into the background drone of the engine. He drove straight passed the two press cars at the crime scene and the cabin and on down to the waterside next to the old boathouse.

Dag went back to the spot where he's stood the day before and Martin followed him.

"Nothing from Bergen, no sign of Johan."

"Did they find anything at the address?"

"They didn't do a search, no, they had no warrant, that's not what we asked for, they just checked to see if he was there."

Dag sighed. "Get on to the office. Get them to do a search. If there's a computer there, a laptop, whatever, I'd like it found."

"Right boss. The office are getting on to the airlines and I had a quick word with Andreas Østrem, he's are computer man. Not that he does everything himself; we use a young guy from Molde University College's IT department as well when we need to."

"This is where the bag containing the memory stick was. Our man threw it into the water there." Dag said pointing.

"Martin frowned. "And you went in and got it out?"

"Not me, no." Dag turned to the boat house and walked towards it. "My young friend hiding inside the boathouse helped me."

There was a scrabbling noise from the boathouse and the door creaked open. Aksel came out.

"This is Aksel," Dag told Martin, "he's been helping us with our inquiries." Dag gave the boy a smile. "So, did you get into trouble with your mother?"

Aksel shrugged. "I said I slipped off a rock and into the water."

"Hmm. I wondered if you could be a bit more help?" The boy nodded and smiled. "I want you to think very carefully about the day you saw the man here at the waterside when he threw that package into the water. Is there anything else you can remember? Think very hard, close your eyes and imaging it all as if it's happening again, like a dream, then tell me again everything you saw."

Aksel closed his eyes and screwed up his face.

"He had a phone."

"Did he make a call or did he get one?"

"I didn't really hear anything. Maybe it just buzzed like my dad's does sometimes."

"And he answered it?"

"Hmm, yes. He didn't speak loud, but he seemed a bit angry."

"Was it a long or short phone call?"

"Just short. That's when he threw that bag into the water. The he just walked off back up the road."

"Ok, that's great, you'll make detective one day! But you'll need to go to school when you're supposed to. You're not there again today."

Aksel smiled and nodded. "They closed the school house today because of what happened, we've all got the day off!"

"Ah, well, just promise me you'll go to school when you're supposed to otherwise you'll never make detective."

Aksel smiled and nodded.

"Uh, oh." Interrupted Martin. "Here come the press."

Two cars were driving down the road towards them.

"OK, let's get going and back to Kristiansund, I'm in no hurry to talk to them, let's leave that to the Chief. Aksel," he said turning to the boy," get back in the boathouse; stay there and keep quiet until those men leave. Don't see or speak to them. And don't tell a word of this to anyone else, eh, this is our secret for the moment."

Aksel nodded eagerly, smiled again, and was off through the boathouse door closing it carefully behind him.

Dag and Martin were quickly into their car and, with Marin back behind the wheel, were off before the press had chance to park and get out of their cars.

5.

It was nearly lunch time before they were back at HQ. Dag was about to go up a flight of stairs to the Chief's office when another officer, coming down and guessing where he was headed, told him that the Chief had gone to some meeting or other and wouldn't be back for a couple of hours. Dag relaxed, brightened and heading back to his own office, an open plan one with his desk at one end, four other desks and a couple of freestanding dividers half way along.

Martin's desk was just in front of his and the two could communicate freely between each other.

"Chief not in?"

"Not for a couple of hours."

"Thought you looked remarkably cheerful. I dropped the memory stick off with Andreas. He took a look at it straight away didn't recognise the file type; didn't think he'd be able to do much so he's called in his young expert hacker."

Dag gave him a worried look.

Martin shrugged. "Anyone expert in these sort of things is probably the sort of guy that can do that sort of thing. Ole Forsberg's his name."

"Better to give them official work I suppose." Mumbled Dag.

"We're getting off a search warrant for Bergen now. They've promised to do what they can; suggested tomorrow morning."

Dag had sat behind his desk. "I'll give an old friend a call. I'd like them to do it this afternoon. As soon as you get word that the warrant's been issued, let me know."

At that moment a DC, the only other person occupying a desk came around a divider. "Report from an airline Sir, Wideroe, they've got a match on that passenger, Johan Christiansen, boarded a 13.05 flight to Bergen on the 26th." She said.

"Just three days after resigning from his job." Commented Dag. "Didn't waste much time. Either he had something else arrange well before hand, what with needing accommodation and everything, or it was done in some haste. Martin, try and find out about where he was staying, was a rented, an apartment, a room, who's the landlord and when did he arrange it?"

Martin just nodded his understanding and started to make some calls. He could get the owners information from Bergen City Council, hopefully with a contact number. If not it shouldn't be too hard to find out, everything was sat one's finger tips these days; saved a awful lot of legwork.

Dag's phone rang and he answered. He anticipated it being the Chief, but it wasn't. Bjorn was calling from the forensics department. He listened and then said that he'd go and to his office.

"Bjorn's got something. His assistant had put it away in an evidence bag not thinking it important. I'm going over to have a look. And I'll probably skip off and have some lunch as well. See you after." He told Martin.

Forensics was at the far rear of the building but it didn't take Dag long to get there.

"So what's this you found?"

"Nothing much really. Just a small piece of paper. Here." He said showing Dag a small plastic evidence bag with it in. "And I saw the Chief's car turning up at the back. Thought you might like a short break from the office."

Dag gave him a look and at the same time glanced out of the window and saw the Chief's car parked.

"Thanks." Inside the bag was a small strip of paper. On it was written, neatly, two numbers each of six digits – 781234 567897. "A code, or a password for something, may be to log on to an internet account, a bank account maybe."

Dag took out his note book and wrote the number down. "You can put it with the rest of the evidence." He thought for a moment. "It might unlock a computer, or even maybe a data file?"

Bjorn shrugged. "Who knows, it could be for almost anything."

Dag nodded. "OK well thanks for that – and the other. I think I'll take a short lunch break."

The Chief when he called Dag's phone was not impressed that Martin answered it and told him that Dag had gone out. He left a message on Dag's mobile, as Dag didn't answer immediately, telling him to come back in a.s.a.p.

Dag was only away for half an hour. Martin was all too ready to speak to him when he came back. Before he could say anything he raised his hand and said, "I know the Chief want to see me immediately."

"Just before you go, boss, I've something. The apartment that was rented out was done online through Roomlet. But it wasn't rented out to our Johan Christiansen. It was rented out to someone called Markus Dagestad who took the keys on the 26th at about 16.00. That would fit in with our man. He left two days ago."

"Hmm, using a false name perhaps or maybe someone booked it for him? And he left two days ago, when the murder took place?" Dag mused.

"Sir!" said the DC as she came around the divider. "Something else for you. I check out the airlines at Bergen, and I asked them to extend the data search to today."

"Good thinking, you're learning – both of you."

"Johan Christiansen boarded a Norwegian Air flight two days ago at 19.10 hours to London Gatwick."

"Really!" said Dag raising his eyebrows.

""Could he be our man, boss? Could he have been the murderer? It would make sense. If he came back to the village, had an argument over something and killed him. Then back to Bergen and run away to London."

"Except that he doesn't appear on any other flight. And the only likely way he'd get back to the village and away again would be to fly. No, I don't think he's our man, even if it looks like it." He made ready to go to see the Chief. "But I'll certainly mention it to the Chief, it might give him a hope that this will all pan out easily for him."

His interview with the Chief took some time. He went through everything he thought was necessary, although may have misremembered one or two elements, telling himself that he could make sure that all the details were recorded when he put pen to paper and it was juts tiredness that had affected his recall. But he made sure that he told the Chief all about Johan Christiansen. The Chief nodded knowingly and told him to do what he could to trace him. At least he could tell the press that they had some sort of lead and that it was likely it could have been a local argument or accident. However, he had to tell Dag that KRIPOS, National Criminal Investigation Service had already taken an interest and was sending two investigators from Oslo. Although they weren't likely to be there until the next afternoon. It would probably mean he only had until then to make any further investigations before the whole affair was taken out of their hands.

Dag said he would do what he could, but they may not find out much more before the team arrived. The Chief merely shrugged and told him to do what he could. By tomorrow morning they wouldn't be using up his resources and budgets on the case, Oslo would be.

"Is there any way of tracing Johan Christiansen at the UK end?"

Martin smiled. "I've got a friend in immigration. He's got some contacts in the UK immigration service. They've promised to check out the flight arrivals."

"You seem to have rather a lot of useful contacts Martin. I'll have to make a note."

"Anything else?"

"Bergen had a chat with the owner of the apartment. He recognised the photo of Johan Christiansen and said it was of the renter Markus Dagestad."

"So, he was using an assumed name."

"Anything on the memory stick yet?"

"Not yet."

"Think I'll go down and see what they've found out. Which office is it?"

"Zero one four."

"The basement?"

Martin nodded.

"That's how important they think modern technology is, eh?"

Dag knocked on the door and opened it. It was a small office and crowded with various computers on two desks and a small computer workstation. Two young men sat at the workstation. They turned as dag entered. The one on the left moved to stand.

"No need to get up." Dag told them. He looked at their pale faces; they didn't look as if they'd left college yet and dressed as if they still did.

The one on the left stood up anyway. "Sir."

Now he looked at the young man he realised that he wasn't just pale he was white, and so were his lips. Dag knew that it was a sign that something was wrong. He was nervous and rubbing his hands. Even though the room was cold, the young man was sweating. His compatriot, obviously the external hacker didn't look any more comfortable.

Dag gave him a hard stare. "What's the problem?"

The young man, Andreas Østrem, took a deep breath. "It's the memory stick Sir."

Dag nodded. "You had a look at it I believe?"

"Yes, when DS Sorensen gave it to me. It wasn't a file I could recognise or open."

"Ole here came a few minutes ago to take a look."

Dag nodded to him. "And?"

"Something's happened Sir."

Dag's eyes narrowed. "Something? What sort of something?"

"The memory stick; I could have sworn it was the same one. I only left the office for a few minutes, to collect Ole from reception and book him in."

There was a solid silence for a moment.

Dag felt his stomach tighten. "You left the memory stick here in the office. Did you lock the door?"

Andreas slowly nodded on the negative. "We're in the basement of a police station, Sir. I didn't think I needed to. I mean, its secure here isn't it?"

"Then what's on that memory stick you're looking at?"

"Music Sir, just music. Nothing else at all. And we can tell it's a different stick."

"Shit." Was all Dag could say. He took a deep breath. I want you to write a report, a detailed one, now. "Get it up to me, or if I'm not there Martin Sorensen, no-one else. Do you understand? And for now keep this to yourself. Not a word to anyone. If it was someone in this Station I don't want to tip them off. If someone's come in from outside we've got to find them."

With that he was out of the door and leaping up the stairs back to his office.

"Martin, a word." He said as he grabbed Martin's wrist and took his away to a quiet corner and told him what had happened. "Find a reason to look at the reception CCTV. I want a list of everyone coming and going over the last few hours. Do it now!" And Martin walked briskly away to do his bidding.

Dag was back at his desk. Martin's phone rang and Dag diverted the call to his own. It was Martin's friend in immigration. He had managed to pull a favour incredibly quickly. As the flight and thimefor the gate was known the British had been able to check the passengers who had gone through immigration control quite quickly. There was no sign of a Johan Christiansen having landed. Dag asked if there was any chance of another favour; could they check for a Markus Dagestad. The friend said he could try, but he was just about all out of favours for the moment.

Dag wasn't too concerned. He was sure that , if they checked, they would find the second name. Johan was obviously using a second passport.

There were a couple of reasons Dag could think of for Johan using a false name. He could, of course, have been directly involved in the murder, but Dag had already discounted that. He must certainly had some knowledge of what had happened and was at least indirectly involved. And if he had some involvement or knowledge of it what were the reasons for his 'escape' One was that he was being forced or coerced to leave, the other that he was escaping any consequences of what might befall him, suffering the same fate as the murdered man. Either was possible. Whichever it was Johan was the key to the enquiry; the only significant key now that the memory stick was missing, or rather, stolen.

Martin retuned from his task.

"Not much to check through since 0800. Mostly staff. A few visitors going to various offices, all apparently legitimate it seems. There's just one that stands out." Martin paused. You haven't had a visitor yourself have you boss?"

"You'd know if I had."

"Then I think that's our man. He showed ID and signed in, said he was coming to meet with you."

Dag had been tapping a pen on his desk, but stopped. "And who was this mystery visitor?"

"Signed in as Jan Haaland. His ID said he was from ..." Martin read his notebook "... E-tjenesten."

"E-tjenesten! That's Military Intelligence. Real or fake?"

Martin shrugged. Has any of us ever seen one of their ID's? We're getting him checked out now."

"That's if they admit to him being one of theirs. If it's something like E14 they'll never verify it. This is definitely going out of our hands, I can tell you that. And KRIPOS are due here tomorrow as well, if it isn't also taken off their hands. I'd loved to have known what was on that stick."

Martin cleared his throat. "Um, well, yes, boss, I think I may have done something I shouldn't have."

"Oh yes, and what is that Martin?" Dag asked with a worried frown.

"When we were looking at the stick on my laptop I think I may have accidently pressed a key and copied it; purely by accident of course."

Dag's face brightened. "Really? Well, accidents do happen don't they? Can we get it down to our experts?"

"I don't think we'll have to , here comes Andreas now." Martin replied as Andreas came sheepishly into the room holding a sheaf of paper.

"Ah, Andreas, your report, thanks for being so quick." Dag took it and pointed to Martin. "Martin here's got something for you to look at."

Martin had already plugged another stick into his laptop and was copying the data.

"Keep it under lock and key or on your person at all times. And remember, for now, not a word."

"He's still here. We'll get on it right away." Andreas told him, looking particularly relieved, and trotted off to his basement.

Dag updated Martin on the call from immigration and told him his thoughts. Martin agreed that Johan must have got himself deep into something he shouldn't have and that he was either on the run afraid for his life or he was being spirited away either with or without his agreement.

"On the other hand." Martin added. "What if he didn't get on the plane at all. What if someone else did in his place; what if the computerised boarding system is incorrect? That would open up another alternative."

"That either he or someone else wants us to think he's left for London, but he could still be in Norway." Dag thought out loud. He shook his head. Too many possibilities. It's making things more difficult not easier. Let's assume, one he's in London, and therefore we're not likely to find him; that'll have to left to

KRIPOS, or perhaps he is still in Norway; that we can check out somehow. Can we get his bank details? Perhaps his cards have been used in the last day or two."

"I can try, but that'll be difficult, you know how the banks are."

Dag's phone rang. It was his contact in Bergen. He listened then thanked him.

"Nothing to go on at the apartment. He'd cleared out."

"Did the apartment have wifi?" Martin asked him.

"I imagine so."

"There may be a way of checking what his usage was when he was there with the provider. I can't say I know that much about it. I'll ask Andreas, he'll know. I need to stretch my legs anyway, I'll pop down and see him."

"Let me know straight away of they've found out anything."

Dag heard a commotion outside the building. He looked down from his second floor window and saw the Chief below standing in front of a small group of reporters and a TV camera crew. 'He'll be watching himself on TV tonight and honing his PR skills.' Smiled Dag.

He watched the small circus for a while and thought. Then he turned and spoke to DC. "Jenny, you any good on computers? Of course you are, all you youngsters are. There's something I'd like you to do. There's a chemical plant near the murder scene. It seemed to be of particular interest to our missing body. And Johan Christiansen worked there. I know they produce methanol but I need to know what methanol is used for. The only thing I can think of is antifreeze. But there must be something more important than that, something more interesting. Have a look on the web will you?"

Jenny gave him an eager smile and set to work behind her screen. "Right away Sir."

He looked back out of the window. The crowd had dispersed expect for two men hoping against hope for any further information. The Chief must have come back inside.

"I'm just off to see the Chief." Dag told Jenny.

He told the Chief of the unexpected visit from a likely member of military intelligence and the loss of, or rather, exchange of, the memory stick. The Chiefs face went stony white. "Are you sure? No-one's told me or warned me."

"This is the first chance I've had to tell you. We're checking it out right now. In a way I hope it is our military friends. If, not, then it's even more of a problem. God knows what KRIPOS will say if it isn't. Mind you, will E-tjenesten admit to it? Either way …"Dag shrugged and left it hanging.

The chief sat back and took a deep breath. "I'm glad I didn't know this before the press interview. At least I told them the truth as I saw it then." He sat with his finger forming a bridge, thinking. "I think things have gone far enough for the moment. We're going to have to back off."

"Hmm. That's all very well and good if the visitor was who he said he was; but if he wasn't then we have to carry on and investigate. If we don't there'll be other questions from KRIPOS."

Unhappily the Chief had to agree, but only to carry on with any investigations if the visitor's credentials weren't verified.

Dag returned to his office to find out if that was case.

"Anything on our spy?" Dag asked Martin who had just returned from the basement.

"I'll check now. As far as the data is concerned they've got as far as getting a message asking for a password; which could, of course, be anything."

"Hmm, I've got something they may try." Dag told him. "I'll give Andreas a call."

"Oh, and as far as the internet provider to the apartment's concerned we would have to find out his IP address, and that might be almost impossible."

Dag called Andreas. "I've got a couple, of numbers that were found on some paper found at the victim's cabin. They look like codes, possibly passwords."

Dag told him and quietly reeled off the two numbers. Andreas said he'd give them a go. Dag stayed on the phone whilst he and Ole tried them.

"No luck." Andreas told him. "Not as they are anyway. Must be for something else. Could be almost anything, any internet account, maybe a bank account. Might also be something physical, a lock perhaps?" Andrea suggested.

"A lock, eh. Yes that's possible. Thanks Andreas, let me know if you have any luck with that data." And Dag finished the call.

He started tapping the pen again on his desk. He was thinking.

"Martin?" Dag asked. Martin looked up at him as he put down his phone. "If you were travelling and didn't want to take anything incriminating with you what would you do with it?"

Martin shrugged. "Put it away somewhere safe to pick up when I needed to."

"Exactly. A deposit box maybe, or a left luggage office or facility. And where would that be? At a railway station or airport I would think. No, maybe not, all you get for one of those is a key as far as I'm aware; it's not a combination lock." He answered his own question. "Anything to report?" He asked having noted that Martin had just finished a call.

"The visitor. The Ministry are being very tight lipped as we suspected. I think we'll need the Chief to make some calls."

Dag nodded. "I'll tell him."

The Chief was less than happy. But he realised that no-one at the Ministry was likely to talk to anyone at less than his rank so he made a couple of calls. It was half an hour before he got back to Dag. They could not confirm the existence of the visitor. The wording was not in the least helpful. It still left the matter open, not saying whether he was one of theirs or wasn't. They had told him of their intention to be at the station the next day, by lunchtime. They were keeping things close to their chests and making sure their arrival preceded KRIPOS. There was no doubt they were intent on taking control of the situation, which at least got the matter off the Chief's books but gave Dag even less time to uncover anything else.

As he returned to his office Jenny caught his attention.

"Yes, Jenny, what have you found out?"

She held a sheet of paper and looked at it. "The methanol, Sir, it's mostly used for very ordinary chemical processes, and for antifreeze like you said. But there's been some new stuff on line lately. It's being used in some new types of batteries. They've been designed out in the Far East but the tech has been offered to the Americans. The batteries are really efficient and reduce emissions. There's a report that says the military have developed them for use in battlefield equipment, and for use on some underwater drones they're developing. Not much about that. But they reckon they will be very quiet and difficult to detect. Thought you'd be interested." She looked at him to see his reaction.

"Hmm, very interesting Jenny, well done."

Dag turned to Martin. "Well, now, that explains our Military friend's interest in all this. And puts it well out of our league. But a murder is still a murder. And until I'm told otherwise, we carry on with the investigation."

Dag tapped his pen on the desk and looked at his watch. It was 15.30.

"Times getting on Martin. I think we'll take a ride out to the airport. It's the nearest place with any left luggage facility. If that's what the numbers are about, that's where we need to go. I can't think of anything else."

It took no more than ten minutes to get there, passing the new Joint Police HQ that was still under construction on the way.

They had both travelled from the airport before. It was only small and neither of them could remember having seen any left luggage lock-ups when they'd been there before. And now they stood in the main entrance they could see there were none. So they headed for the main information desk.

They showed their ID's and asked what would happen if someone wanted to leave some luggage. The woman said that they rarely got asked that, but if they did they would give them a ticket and put the case in the back office until the passenger returned.

"And do you get anyone not coming back for their case?"

"Sometimes, usually if it's something small and someone's got their flight and can't be bothered with it."

"And what do you do with it then?"

"It goes to lost property if we've had it a week or so, sometimes longer."

"And do you have anything at the moment, that hasn't been claimed?"

"I don't think so; I'll go and have a look."

She was only away for a couple of minutes and retuned holding a brief case. "There's this, I forgot about it, it was put down beside a desk in the corner. It must have been here for a week."

"Dag pulled out his handkerchief. "Thanks, I wish you had just told us and not handled it. Never Mind. He took it off her. "We'll take this. Do you want me to sign anything?"

"Oh, I'm sorry, I suppose you'd better, I've got a receipt book somewhere."

Dag and Martin looked at the case. Dag felt its weight. It was heavy. It must have been made of solid steel. Either side of the handle there were two locks, or each lock had a tumbler of numbers; two combination locks.

"It looks like we may have hit the jackpot." Said Dag.

Back at the car, having signed the receipt. Dag placed the case carefully on the back seat.

"We'll get this straight over to Bjorn to take a look at and check for prints before anyone opens it. But I'm pretty sure the numbers will get us in."

Bjorn had left early so Dag had to decide whether or not to open the case. He decided that, as long as he was careful and didn't wipe any prints, he'd take the chance.

He got his note of the numbers. Carefully with one index finger he turned the first of the tumblers to match the first number and then the second. He put his thumbs on the two sliders that operated the locks and pulled them. The lid of the case clicked open. He lifted the lid and he and Martin looked inside.

There were sheets of paper, mostly typewritten with diagrams drawn on them, sat on a red colours folder. But on top of it all were two other documents. Each was a passport. Neither was Norwegian. They could easily see that one was from the UK but the other was one they did not immediately recognise. Dag put on a pair rubber gloves and picked it up.

"Lithuania. That's unusual."

He closed the lid. "I think we'll leave this for tomorrow's visitors. We've had a long day or two; I think we need a break, go home have a rest. And be back here early tomorrow?" He suggested.

"I've still got the report writing to do."

"You can take your laptop can't you?"

"Take my work home? Yes, I suppose I can."

"I'll see you bright and early tomorrow morning them; say 0730?"

"Martin nodded less than enthusiastically. "OK boss."

6.

The wind had picked up that morning and had veered to the south west. Clouds were forming and were a precursor to the rain that must be on its way across the Atlantic. Dag and Martin parked their cars at the same time and walked to the office together.

"Report written?"

"All done."

"Let's get some hot strong coffee first and have a think."

They settled either side of Dag's desk with hot mugs of coffee.

"The spooks will be here by lunchtime. They'll be flying up I'm sure. Could be here earlier. The earliest flight from Oslo gets in at 0845, I checked. The next one wouldn't be until 14.40. I think they'll want to surprise us with an early arrival."

"They'll be here by ten then?"

"Gives us a couple of hours. But I can't think of much else we can do. They'll take over the case and remove all the evidence. The murder itself will be passed to KRIPOS but that'll just be a formality I'm sure."

"Kripos were supposed to be here after lunch?"

"If they're not the early flight they'll be on the later one. Mind you, that's if they come at all. It's entirely possible that they've already been sidelined and won't need to come."

"So what is there left for us to do?"

"Well, if we don't have the murder, we at least have another case."

"Which is?"

"Our missing nephew, Johan Christiansen. We can put that through as a missing person's case."

"But he's probably in the UK by now."

"Maybe, maybe not, that's something we're not sure of. And it's something we can be working on. Is there any way we can get his bank details? Maybe his uncle has them he's left a bank statement somewhere. At his uncle's perhaps. We need to know if he's using his card. Get the usual paperwork ready for the banks or the specific one when you find out which one." "Actually," he added, "the personnel department at the chemical plant must have been paying him directly to his bank account. Put some pressure on them, they must know the details."

DC Jenny Strøm arrived and Martin briefed her on getting the paperwork ready for the banks then started making his phone calls.

Dag interrupted him. "Not heard anything from Andreas and his friend have you?"

"No Sir."

I'll pop down and see what they're up to."

Both Andreas and Ole were in the basement office reclining in their swivel chairs watching a flickering computer screen. They turned as Dag entered.

"Anything?" he asked them.

Andreas shook his head. "Nothing. It's been running all night. I would have got a ping if there had been anything. It can take days and then nothing. We've not got the most up to date and fastest machines, you know."

"Hmm. Well, you don't have much more time. Some men from one of the Government Ministries are due in. They'll be taking over."

Andreas and Ole looked at one another. "Which one exactly?" Ole asked.

"Defence; Military Intelligence."

Ole's face darkened and he turned a little pale. "Perhaps we'd better just pack in now." He said looking at Andreas. "I don't want my programme running when they get here."

Dag shook his head. "I don't think I want to know what you're suggesting. They should be here by ten so after that I'd suggest you stop and skedaddle out of here; along with your programme."

Dag returned to his office and at 10.00 on the dot the men from the Ministry arrived at reception. They were shown to the Chief's office and Dag was called up to it as well.

Three chairs had been place before the Chief's desk. The two to the left were taken. The chief indicated that Dag should take the third. He sat, looked over to the two dark suited men and gave a brief nod. The one next to him nodded back and said, "Good morning Detective Inspector Meldel." And then turned back to face the Chief.

Clearly the Chief was expected to be the one to speak.

"These are agents Rolf and Roar from E-tjenesten – department E14 in fact. They will be taking over the murder case. If you wouldn't mind Inspector I'd like you to arrange all the evidence to be put together – I imagine everything is bagged, logged and accounted for – and sign it over to them. "

"I'll arrange it with forensics, everything is with them. With one exception, that is."

The Chief raised an eyebrow and the agent next to him turned and gave him a piercing look.

"Although the memory stick was taken or stolen, by someone assumed to be from a Ministry Department, it was inadvertently copied when being looked at by our computer expert. Fortunately, purely by error, it exists on a laptop in his office."

Dag could see and almost see a sense of relief from the agent, whereas the Chief was growing a bright red.

"You said nothing about this before!"

"I was in the office just before coming here. We have only just discovered the error. I would have come here and told you straight away if I wasn't already on my way as requested."

The Chief frowned at him. He knew exactly how Dag felt by his tone.

"That's excellent news!" said the agent. "Very fortuitous, shall we say. Who has looked at it?"

"Myself and my Sergeant had a look and, of course, our expert. Unfortunately it seems to be an odd type of file, it couldn't be accessed."

"Good." Said Rolf, for that was who spoke. "Let's keep it that way."

Rolf turned to the Chief. "If we may I'd like to get my hands on that computer first, then the rest of the evidence."

"Certainly." agreed the Chief.

"Is it on a desktop or a laptop?" Rolf asked Dag.

"A laptop." Dag told him. "And there's a briefcase we think is connected. We picked it up late yesterday at the airport."

The Chief glared at Dag and raised his eyes to the ceiling before saying through his teeth, "A briefcase?"

"Yes, it was just a hunch. The guy was travelling with virtually nothing. I just thought it might be likely that he could have left something at the airport if he'd flown here. We checked it out when we finished work yesterday. A briefcase had been left and not picked up. It's pretty heavy – steel I would think – it's got two combination locks."

"Did you try opening it?" asked Rolf.

"Try? Well, there again we had a bit of luck. Forensics had picked up a small slip of paper. On it was two sets of six digits; exactly what was needed to open the case."

"And you opened it."

"Natural curiosity of a Police Inspector – yes."

"And?"

"Paperwork and a file. We didn't take a close look. But on top were two passports."

"And you had a look at those I suppose?"

"One British the other Lithuanian."

"I think Chief Inspector," Rolf said turning to him, "we need to take it as read that our Inspector here, and any colleagues, makes no record of what they saw."

"I agree." The Chief said with a hard edge to his voice. "You've heard that D.I. Meldel, you can take that as an order from me."

"Of course Sir, no problem." Dag said pleasantly and turned to give Rolf a smile of agreement.

"Good." Rolf nodded. "Shall we go? First let's get that laptop.""

They rose and left the Chief with nothing else to say. Once through the door and in the corridor Dag moved in front of them to show them the way.

"The basement you said?" asked Rolf.

"And when you've finished," the Chief spoke out, "I'd like to have a word with you."

"Yes Sir." Dag replied as they were leaving. "We'll take the stairs, won't take long." Dag told his guests. Dag hoped it would give them a time so that Ole could be out of the way and Andreas ready for them.

Dag knocked on Andreas' door and waited for it to unlock and open hoping to show that they had a modicum of security. Andres let them in and Dag was relieved to see that Ole had gone.

"Can you help you Sir?" Andreas asked Dag as if he had no idea why they were there or who his guests were.

Dag explained that these were men from the Defence Ministry and they would need to look at the laptop with the memory stick's data on. Andreas showed them over to the laptop.

"That's the one."

Rolf nodded to his compatriot, Roar. "Well be taking that with us." He aid as Roar immediately went to work unplugging it.

"Hey, what the hell are you doing!" protested Andreas. "There's confidential stuff on there, all my files, programmes I use. Data, stuff I can't possibly replace. You can't just unplug it and take it! Sir, please!" he pleaded with Dag.

"Sorry Andreas, it's out of my hands. Orders are orders. There's no way I can stop them."

Andreas gaped and slumped into his swivel chair, staring blindly at the men.

"This can't be happening, it'll take months of work to get everything back together." He moaned.

Roar had the laptop under his arm.

"Now for the rest of the evidence, if you don't mind Inspector."

Dag nodded. "I'll take you to forensics. Bjorn will be expecting you."

As they left, before closing the door behind him, Dag turned round and gave Andreas a sideways grin.

Bjorn was waiting for them. All the evidence had been placed in a single larger mail style bag. He was holding the paperwork for it ready to be signed.

"Here you go." He said. "It's all yours. Everything's listed. I've got a draft report if you want a copy. The final report won't be ready until tomorrow. I've got other things to do."

"No problem." Rolf told him. "I'll give the D.I. an email address to send it to. We'll be conducting our own full investigation anyway and our own report."

Bjorn held out the paperwork for him to sign and he scribbled a signature on it.

"All yours then."

"I'll escort you out." Dag offered.

"Our plane's at 15.05. We'll go straight back to the airport. If you could provide a car?"

"Not hanging around then? I'm sure we can manage that."

They were seated in the reception area whilst Dag arranged for a car then Dag joined them.

"There's just one thing I'd like to clear up."

Rolf gave him a questioning look. "Which is?"

"Johan Christiansen; he appears to have flown to the UK."

"So we also believe. He will be traced. Our friends in the UK are helping with our enquiries."

"But he didn't land there."

Rolf gave him an intense stare and there was a moment's silence. "What do you mean?"

"My DS pulled a few strings, he's got some friends in the right places, and he asked the right questions. According to UK immigration no-one by the name of Johan Christiansen passed through immigration around the time of the flights arrival."

Rolf's steel-blue eyes, as steely as his stare, held on to Dag's. "I see. That's interesting."

"There was another name cropped up, could be an alias, Petter Johansen."

Rolf looked away, thinking. "That's very useful information D.I. Meldel. I thank you for that."

"You can call me Dag, seeing as I only know you as Rolf."

Rolf turned back to him and gave a brief smile. "Of course, Dag."

"The thing is," Dag continued, "has Johan left Norway or not. Everything gives the appearance that he has. But ... I tend to get feelings, intuitions about things, a gut feeling if you like; and I'm not convinced."

"Hmm, an interesting hypothesis. And how do your feelings, your instinct, usually turn out Dag?"

"Usually more success than failure."

"I see."

"The thing is, as a result we've logged Johan as a missing person."

Rolf looked at him again for a couple of seconds. "You're suggesting that you are still pursuing the case."

"No, I'm saying that we are conducting enquires on a related but differed matter."

Rolf leaned back into the chair and was silent again, and then spoke.

"This case load is going to be quite heavy for us. We've got limited resources – haven't we all. I'm not sure I have the means at the moment to pursue the possibility that Johan is still in Norway. However, if he is, we need to know, and as a matter of importance. I'll tell you what I'll do Dag. I'll allow you to investigate the whereabouts of Johan, but I insist that you keep me informed at all times as to what you're doing and what you've found out; keep nothing back. I'll give you a contact number as well as the email address you'll need."

"I'm not so sure my Chief will see it that way. He won't want to use any more of his budgets on this"

Rolf smiled. "I think I can arrange for someone to whisper a quiet word in your Chief's ear. The thought of some brownie points helping us should persuade him."

Dag smiled and nodded. "Very well then. We'll concentrate on what happened to Johan."

"And if you find him or get near to him I want him safe and sound. I don't want anything unfortunate happening to him, do you understand?"

Dag nodded seriously. "I think I'm aware that if he's on the run his life is probably in danger."

"Good. Here," he passed Dag a card. "The phone number and email address."

"Methanol." Said Dag. "A pretty innocuous chemical for all this fuss."

"One might think so."

"I had a look on the internet. Some odd bits of up-to-date info would say it was less so."

Rolf frowned. "There are some new uses for it, yes."

"Batteries and the like?"

"If you've had a good look then it doesn't take a genius to find out that the military are interested in them. But I'm afraid I'll have to leave it at that. You wouldn't expect any more from me would you?"

"Of course not."

At that moment an officer came up to announce that the car was outside ready to take the guests back to the airport. As the agents got up to leave Rolf came close to Dag and said in a low voice, "If you hit any real problems, find yourself in any serious trouble, use the codeword Arcturus, we'll respond as immediately as we can." Dag felt the knot in his stomach tighten again. With that they left and Dag climbed back up the stairs to the Chief's office as instructed.

"D.I. Meldel," The Chief said glaring at him from behind his desk. The chairs had been moved to one side and Dag stood before him. "I expect to be kept properly informed of the details of cases such as this. I do not expect you to delay telling me things that could put me in an awkward and potentially embarrassing position. I might easily have given completely the wrong information to the press, and what would that look like; what sort of impression would that have given the public, let alone damaging the public's trust in us. And how did it look in front of our guests? It could have looked as if I had no idea what was going on."

"Sir, as I explained, it all came together at the last minute, there was no real chance of briefing you before they turned up, and prior to that there was no substantial evidence that you could have given to the press. I'd have thought that you and our guests would have been happy that that was the case."

"Be that as it may, Inspector, in future I wish to be kept fully informed on matters relating to such cases. We can't allow ourselves to give mixed or erroneous briefings to the press, public or, of course, our superiors. In future you will keep that in the forefront of your mind."

"Of course Sir, absolutely."

"Good. I'm glad we both see it that way. And now you can get on with whatever other cases you have. It's out of our hands now. Oh, and by the way KRIPOS have cancelled. Our Ministry friends must have made a few phone calls. At least we're not going to be bothered by them."

"Some good news then Sir. We've got a couple of other outstanding cases. We'll move on to them."

"That'll be all."

Dag left thinking it could have been worse and knowing that one of the other cases would now be the disappearance of Johan Christiansen.

It was only an hour later that the Chief called him back to his office.

"You seem to be taking up a good deal of my time D.I. Meldel. I've had a call from the Politimester. He has received a request from E14. They have asked that you be assigned to a case." He gave Dag a suspicious look. "You must have made some sort of impression on them. They asked that you be assigned to find our missing man Johan Christiansen. They don't believe he's flown the nest and gone to England. They've cited the fact they are short of manpower to conduct an enquiry. As if we are any better off than them. More likely their budgets are constrained. Why they think our budgets are any better off I don't know. Anyway, the Politimester has told me to provide full cooperation; it's come to him from the Assistant Police Director, so therefore I must, even if it means a couple of hours on a spreadsheet. So, off you go, and remember, keep me fully informed at all times. I don't expect to be kept out of the loop."

He turned away to his computer screen and dag thanked him and left.

Dag let Martin know everything that had transpired and that their missing person's case was official. Not only official, but being supported at the highest level.

Maybe there was some more information they could glean from Johan's family in the village but Dag didn't want his and Martin's time tied up again there. This was a job for Jenny – her first job out on her own gathering what information she thought might be relevant. Dag briefed her. She smiled broadly, a real task last least, she'd find out all she could about Johan, she was sure of it. She'd start out the next morning.

Dag could think of only one other thing to do. There was little more they could find out here; they would have to go to Bergen. It might mean stepping on a few toes in Bergen force, but his old friend there could probably smooth their way.

"Martin, book a couple of tickets to Bergen for tomorrow morning. And see if you can get us some accommodation; one star mind, not five. We'll get the first flight if we can. Find out what time it is."

Martin clicked away on his laptop. "08.45's the earliest. We're luck there's a few seats left."

7.

They met at the airport at 07.15.

"A bit of luck with the accommodation, boss."

"Got somewhere cheap I hope. I can imagine the Chief's face when he sees the expenses."

"Thought I'd check our Roomlet, like our friend Johan did. Found a place straight away. Only one bedroom, but there's a sofa bed in the lounge."

"That'll do nicely – for you."

Martin smiled.

"But even better than that, you'll never guess where I've managed to book."

Dag gave him a blank look.

"Our friend Johan's apartment. Thought I'd give it a try and it was available."

Dag smiled back. "Well done Martin, Good thinking. That could turn out to be very useful."

They arrived at Bergen airport at 10.00 and were at the apartment by 11.00. It was close to the Railway station on Skivebakken, an old part of Bergen on a steep and narrow ascending hill with not much room for more than one car to drive and none for parking. Tourists would have loved it. The owner was there to meet them with the keys, let them in and showed them quickly around.

As she was about to go Dag produced his ID.

He asked her about her previous guests and in particular Johan, who, she told them, was the last guest she'd had. She had only seen him the once when he arrived; a very pleasant and nice young man; quiet, but he seemed the nervous type. He left a day before his booking was due to end and gave the key to the neighbour. Not that she minded, he'd paid the full price in advance.

Dag thanked her and they settled in. They both then did a thourough search of the place looking in every cupboard, closet and nook and cranny. It was always possible that Johan had left some trace behind. But they found nothing.

As soon as they had done so Jenny called. She had gone as early as she could to the chemical plant and talked to personnel manager, or who passed for one. He'd had to get permission from his head office before he gave her the details of Johan's bank account but now she had them. She text them to Dag and back to the office who had the paperwork ready for the bank so that they could trace its use. Now she was on her way to see the uncle to see if there was anything else she could find out.

"Tell the office to phone me direct as soon as they've got anything on his bank account." Dag told her. "Oh, and well done. Keep up the good work."

"So," asked Martin, "what's our first move?"

Dag was relaxing in a wicker chair. "For the moment, not much. But I need to call my contact here. If you need to do anything for a while take a break. Or, better still, have a look around the area. Maybe talk to any neighbours perhaps, see if they saw or noticed anything unusual; show them a picture of Johan, see if they remember him"

"Ok boss." Martin agreed and headed off.

Dag called his friend in the Bergen Police. They agreed to meet up early in the evening. As far as his friend could tell him there was nothing else that had cropped up regarding Johan, not that they'd spent time checking him out other than making a note of the missing person's report that Kristiansund had passed on.

Dag stood at the window deep in thought. The apartment was on the first floor. He was a step or two back from the pane of glass. A net curtain was hung in front of the bottom half of the window but he could see over it through the upper pane and out into the street.

A man was walking slowly along, up the slope of the road, towards a point where a side road split away. Dag moved slowly to one side to keep an eye on him but keeping back from the window. When the man was on the side opposite the turning he stopped and lit a cigarette. He was of average height, dark hair and dressed in casual ordinary clothes. The sort of person who, if a witness in a case was giving a description, could fit almost any average person; an almost impossible match to make. The man was looking innocent enough but Dag could tell that, every now and then, he would be looking down the road towards the apartment.

Dag took his phone and called Martin. He wanted to know where Martin was. Martin had knocked on a few nearby doors when he had left but other than one old woman everyone else seemed to be out at work. The old lady had noticed nothing. He was now heading towards the railway station – always a good place for a coffee and something to eat at a reasonable price.

Dag told him to make his way back but to head back to the apartment form the higher ground, he could use his phone map to find a way. And he told him to be as inconspicuous as possible, explaining that that someone may have them under observation and he didn't want them spooked. But he didn't want them to suspect that they knew they were being watched; that is if they were. He was not to approach anyone but pass innocently by without noticing them.

With a rumbling stomach Martin began his trek back to the apartment. He was only a few minutes away but to get to the higher ground and come down he'd have to make quite a detour, getting onto an upper road and turning back onto Skivebakken. It took him ten minutes.

He came slowly towards the point where the man was standing. He had yet to reach the turning where the road split. Without warning the man flicked his cigarette to the ground and walked, without looking towards Martin down the road that split away from Skivebakken. Martin made sure that he took no notice and carried on walking to the apartment.

Dag had watched it happen. Although the man had appeared not to have noticed Martin he was sure he had, even if it had only been the sound of his footsteps. Dag considered that, whoever it was, was not an amateur.

"So, we're being watched." Said Martin.

"Yes, but by whom?"

"Our friends from the Ministry?"

"No, they made it quite clear to me that they didn't have the resources for this."

"Oh, so that puts it in the more worrying category."

Dag nodded. "Yes, I think we'll have to be pretty careful I'll send a text to Rolf and let him know. I don't want him complaining that he's being kept out of the loop."

"How about we now get some lunch?" Martin suggested.

"Good idea, how far is the Railway Station?"

"By a direct route only a few minutes."

"All right, let's take a break."

They selected a baguette each, a couple of chocolate cakes and ordered coffee, then sat at the small white tables arranged outside the cafe under a line of grand internal arches.

As they finished Dag got a call from the office. They'd already got some info on Johan's bank account. He'd taken out what cash he could, the maximum allowed for the day evidently, the day before he left the apartment. He'd used a Nordea ATM not far from the other side of the railway station at the Bergen Storsenter shopping mall.

"Paying for things in cash." Dag noted. "A sensible precaution, and it means he's not going to be able to track his debit card use."

"He could still have got on theta flight to the UK."

"Then why is a person or persons unknown taking an interest in us? No, he's here in Norway I'm sure of it. Or not in the UJK at any rate. And what we must now be most careful of is accidently leading someone to him. Why should whoever it is go through all the trouble themselves when they can let us do their work for them? We need to be very careful, Martin."

As they got up to leave Dag got another call from Jenny. He listened and thanked her again for her good work

"Another bit of good news." He told Martin. "Johan's uncle found an old credit card statement. It's likely he had a credit card as well. She getting the office to check it out now."

"She's turning out good, boss."

"Dag smiled. "You'll have to watch yourself Martin. I think I'll take a walk down to the harbour and take a look at the fish market; I've not been there for years."

"I'll tag along if that's OK?"."

"Sure." Dag looked at his watch. It was 14.00. "I'll be meeting my Bergen contact later so I'll hang around town. We'll be passing the Central Police Station on the way down to the harbour."

"I might take a look at the old Bryggen area, I've not been there since I was a child."

Dag nodded. "We'll give each other a call if anything crops up. For now we may as well take it easy." Dag stopped to adjust his shoelace and in doing so took a brief look around and to their rear. "Best keep an eye out on and off. If you see someone familiar make a note but carry on being the tourist."

"I will, boss."

After a stroll around the market stalls lining the docks they split up. If anyone was following them they would have to make the decision which one to follow. Dag guessed it was more likely to be him.

He strolled to the southern wharf side. He remembered coming here as a boy, he must have been just eleven years old, he'd come with his father to visit relatives, an aged aunt and uncle. And he recalled being taken for lunch in a restaurant on the first floor of one of the buildings. It was old and traditional, it has probably been there for a century serving much the same food. He had his favourite; pølse with potatoes and gravy. For a moment he thought he caught the smell of it cooking and couldn't help but look around to see if there was a nearby stall serving the dish. But there wasn't. He wandered along and tried to remember which one, but the exact memory refused to come back to him. And any, the eating places seemed to be international, Subway, Burger King and Thai. At least on the wharf with the markets you could still get a huge variety of Norwegian food and drink.

He went a little further along and stopped for a moment in front of a jeweller's. One of the windows curved inwards towards an inset door. It was at a perfect angle to see a reflection of the way he'd come. He gazed at the items displayed but in truth was inspection the reflection. There had been someone who'd quickly stepped into the door way of the hotel he'd passed. It could be anyone, of course, but he had that feeling in his stomach again. And the brief glimpse of the figure and it's look reminded him of the man watching the apartment.

He could do nothing be aware and keep an eye out. He would keep on the move appearing to wander around like a tourist until he was due to meet his contact. Then he would take a measure or two to shake off anyone that may be following.

About half an hour later, sitting in a cafe having a coffee sitting directly in a window so he got a good view of the street outside he got another call from the office. They had checked out Johan's credit card. He had not used it for many months – until recently. Then, on the same day as he took the cash out, it had been used to buy a railway ticket at Bergen Station. The transaction couldn't tell what ticket was bought or to where but they were checking what tickets were available on that day for that price. They would get back to him.

Dag called Martin and told him.

"So, he's definitely in Norway. He didn't get that flight but got a train somewhere instead."

"Yes." Dag agreed. "And there's only one place he's likely to have gone from Bergen and that's Oslo, but I'll wait till the office confirms it. Yet again he's sensibly trying to keep his movements as hidden as possible."

He didn't have to wait long.

There was only one fare that matched and that was the ticket to Oslo. He bought it at 15.30. The next train to Oslo would have been at 16.15. It's a long journey and wouldn't have arrived until 00.15 that night.

Dag told Martin the news and sent a text to Rolf. Martin had seen enough of the old town and suggested they find somewhere for a drink. Dag suggested a bar on the harbour frontage where he had met his contact before. It had wide windows and they'd have a good view of the road outside.

Screens were showing a British football match but few customers were watching, and only half a dozen were drinking. Which beer to order was a hard choice, they were proud to be advertising over fifty different brews. In the end Dag stuck to his usual Aass Classic, Martin chose Humle-Helvet.

"So." Said Martin. " Does this mean we're off to Oslo?"

"I'll see if Rolf gets back to me. If he's gone there I'd have thought they'd like to take it over rather than us going so far out of our way. And I can just imagine what the Chief's going to say – Oslo expenses!"

They were half way through their drink when Dag's phone rang again. It was Jenny. Again Dag listened, frowned, and thanked her.

"Well, now that changed things again. The office have just noticed that Johan's credit card was used again."

"Do they know what for?"

"A hotel. They probably asked for it as security."

"He's in Oslo then."

"It wasn't used in Oslo. It was used in Voss. At 18.00 hrs after he got the train."

"Ah! So he bought a ticket all the way to Oslo, but jumped the train at Voss."

"And he had to get the 16.15 train. It's the only one then that stops at Voss, the others got through to Oslo without stopping."

"He really is trying to cover his tracks isn't he."

"If he wants to hide from someone there's only two good choices; head for the hills and keep out of site, or mingle in a large city where you're less likely to be noticed. It seems he's taken the first option. I'll update Rolf again. Take a look on that smart phone of yours and check out the train times. I'll want to meet my friend first so after seven."

It was then Dag's phone buzzed. It was Rolf. Rolf asked him to call him, which Dag thought was odd as if he'd texted why didn't he just call. He supposed it was all part of a security procedure so he dialled and called him. Rolf thanked him for all the information so far.

"We've had one problem, though." Rolf told Dag. "The data on the laptop has been deleted. Our guys reckon it was some sort of virus or malware that infected it at the same time as the data was downloaded from the memory stick; caused the data to automatically destroy itself after a certain period of time. So now we are left without the very thing we needed. That makes it more imperative to find Johan Christiansen and find out what he knows. You said that you thought you may be under surveillance? I was concerned that might be so. I think we might find someone to shadow you; very discretely, of course. We'd prefer it if you carried on with the case as if it was a simple missing person's enquiry. But I think it best that we had someone closer to hand. I won't give any more details, the less you know the better. Anyway keep up the good work and keep me informed. Oh, and take care."

With that he hung up.

Dag finished his beer. He sat and thought. He thought and felt that he was being used, and maybe had been since the beginning. He didn't like it. And who was really following them? Was it whoever had stolen the memory stick, whoever had killed the mystery man, or had E14 been tracking them all along? He felt he was being used and might have been from the start. Was he being used as decoy or perhaps a useful target as a trap for whoever E14 were after? it was all possible. Was now the time to mention that there was a copy of the data on Martin's laptop? He thought not. If Rolf's people had lost the data then what was on Martin's laptop was now the only copy besides the original memory stick. He would keep that to himself for now. He could always plead ignorance if necessary and so could Martin; who was to say they hadn't inadvertently copied the memory stick and not known that they had. But was the data still on the laptop?

Dag asked Martin to check. He was carrying it a case, got it out and scanned the files.

"It's still there, no problem."

"If it's still on yours why did it get deleted from the one Rolf took from Andreas? If there was some virus or something downloaded with it, the same would have happened when you downloaded it."

"Ole, his friend the computer hacker." Suggested Martin. "That programme he was running. It was supposed to break the password, what if it did something else as well?"

"So he may not be trustworthy either, if, of course, Rolf is being straight with us."

There was silence as Martin checked out his phone.

"There's a train at two minutes to seven and the next is 20.38." said Martin interrupting his thoughts.

Dag called his friend. Unfortunately he'd been called out on a case. They would have to meet another time. For that matter, there was no particular help he could now give Dag on his search for Johan.

They went back to the apartment. Martin phoned the owner to tell her they had to move on and they were at the train station in time for the 18.58 train to Voss. Marti had already been on his laptop searching for accommodation. Voss was not cheap, the few hotels were expensive, even more so that Bergen. Once again on Roomlet they found a small two bed apartment at a reasonably central location for just 710Kr a night. That should keep the Chief happy, or at least not too unhappy.

The final thing Dag did for the day was to call Jenny. He asked her to talk to Eduard Christiansen again and find out if Johan had any connections with the Voss area; maybe family or friends, perhaps he travelled there on occasion, or did someone else in the village, a relative perhaps have connections with Voss or the area around. If Johan was in hiding somewhere in the Voss district he must have had somewhere he knew where it was safe to hide out.

8.

The Voss police station was across the river from where they were staying. They called there in the morning as a matter of courtesy; explain that they were on a missing person's case. The D.I. they spoke to offered to help if necessary. They thanked him and said that there would probably be no reason as their man was likely to have moved on anyway.

Their next stop was the Hotel where Johan's credit card had been used. It was close to the railway station, an historic building and not cheap.

Dag and Martin showed their ID's to the receptionist.

"We're trying to trace a man who used his credit card to pay for a stay here on the 30th of last month; I've got the card details. We need to check it against your customers." Dag told her.

"I will have to talk to my manager. Our residents details are confidential you know. What with data protection laws I'm not sure that we can match it up for you."

Dag smiled. "Well, if you'd care to talk to your manager I'd be most grateful."

She grabbed some paperwork and, rather haughtily, went through to the adjoining office. Within moments a manger appeared.

"I'm not sure the system will be able to do what you've asked for, Sir. Data protection you know, the two sets of data don't link."

"Well then," Dag smiled. "If you'd be good enough to give us a full list of your residents during the period from the 28th for one week we'll look through it. We can sit in the lobby here and do so if you like. Oh, and I imagine you take passport details where necessary?"

The manager gave a cough and straightened his back. "I don't think there will be any need to do your work in the lobby Sir. I'll see about giving you space in a quiet area where you can work undisturbed. I'll ask the clerk if she can print out a list form the bookings file. And, yes, we do of course make note of any passports."

He turned back into the office. Dag and Martin waited to one side as the receptionist dealt with two residents and a few minutes later the manager re-emerged holding a few sheets of paper. "I'll take you to a room we use for interviews. Would you like some coffee?"

It didn't take long to sift through the names. Johan's was there. He had booked in on the 30th, stayed two nights and left. Dag would have to ask to see his bill and check if he had anything else charged other than the room. Martin scanned down the rest of the names and the notes of their passports. Half the names were Norwegian without any need for passport details; the rest were a variety of nationalities, tourists he imagined, mostly Americans with a scattering of people from the rest of Europe and a few Chinese and South East Asians. He spotted one that was interesting.

"There's a Lithuanian on the list." He told Dag.

"Is there? Interesting."

"But why would someone form a small country like Lithuania be involved?"

Martin thought for a moment and then checked out something on his phone.

"Lithuania borders Russia." He said. "Quite a high proportion of Lithuanians are of Russian descent; not been happy since the Lithuanians broke away from Soviet control. And there's a Russian enclave on the coast, Kaliningrad. There's a fair Russian military presence there. And all land movement has to go through Lithuania; and now they are members of NATO which has upset the Russians."

"Hmm, I'm getting to like this less and less. What was the Lithuanian's name?"

"Vaižgantas Svilas. He could just as easily be Russian of course."

"Of course. Let's have another word with reception, see what they remember about Johan, and about Vaižgantas Svilas."

The current receptionist, nor the manager, remembered anything of either man and didn't think she was on duty at the time. They would have to return in the afternoon when the next shift came on; maybe one of them would remember.

There was little else for them to do but wander around Voss and stop for a coffee waiting for Jenny to get back to them and for the afternoon shift change over.

It was 13.30 when they decided to go back to the hotel and when Jenny made her call to them. She seemed to get on well with Eduard and he was more than forthcoming with her. He had taken time to think about her question and called her back. There was a relative, no more than a second cousin of Johan's, who lived some distance from 13TH. He was about the same age. He worked in the small, but renowned, mountain village of Flåm. His name was Jørgen Arnesen. Eduard believed he worked at a hotel there.

"So, next stop Flåm?" Martin asked.

Dag looked at his watch. "Tomorrow I think. There's a train that goes through the mountains to Flåm, it's quite a journey through the mountains, we can catch it tomorrow. Let's go back and talk to the hotel staff."

The staff were not much help; neither the duty receptionist nor the deputy manager could remember anything about Johan, although the receptionist did recall Vaižgantas Svilas. It was the first time a Lithuanian had stayed at the hotel. Dag asked her for a description but she was rather vague, so many people came and went she wasn't sure of any details. So Dag, noticing the CCTV, asked the manager if they still had a copy of the recording for the day that Vaižgantas Svilas. He did. And they went to a back office to trawl through it.

It didn't take too long as they knew the date and time. Now they had a picture of the man and the hotel was able to print it off. Dag got them to do an electronic copy as well so he could send it to Rolf.

He was average height with dark slightly wavy hair and thick lips, but otherwise unremarkable and was dressed casually in a non-descript style. One could pass him in the street without taking any notice whatsoever. But it gave Dag a niggling recognition. Was this the man who had been watching their apartment in Bergen and who he'd though he had a fleeting glimpse of at the harbour side? It was possible. Dag had that feeling in his stomach again. He needed a strong coffee.

The first train was at 10.00 the next morning. They would have to change at Myrdal arriving at Flåm at 14.00. There were only two sizeable hotels in the small town, more a large village really, all equally expensive, besides some smaller pensions and apartments. It shouldn't take them long to find out which one of the hotels Johan's cousin worked at, unless he was employed somewhere further out. The only place that had space available for Dag and Marti was a hostel on the outskirts Flåm, but at least it was the cheapest choice.

They got to the station in good time and bought some newspapers, sandwiches and drinks to take with them. All the time they were keeping a surreptitious eye out for anyone that looked like their stalker. Almost any number of travellers could match his description and it was impossible to detect if any of them had an interest in Dag and Martin. They boarded the train and took seat at one end of a carriage that gave them a view of people coming and going at the far end before, hopefully, anyone would spot them, and anyone passing through the door next to them the going the other way would be spotted before they themselves were.

At Myrdal they had to change platforms. It was another good opportunity to see which passengers did the same – which many of them did. But still no definite sign of anyone shadowing them, either the one from Bergen or, possibly, one of Rolf's men.

They got to Flåm at exactly the appointed time.

There were two hotels close to the station. They only needed to go to the first to find out where Jørgen Arnesen, Johan's cousin worked. It was not there, however, but the other prominent hotel overlooking the main car park on the harbour where local ferries and boats as well as large cruise ships anchored at the head of the Aurlandsfjorden which snaked its way from the main artery of the great Sognefjorden some two hundred kilometres from the North Sea.

Dag and Martin showed their ID's to the woman behind the reception desk.

"We're looking for Jørgen Arnesen, we believe he works here." Dag asked her.

The woman raised an eyebrow behind her glasses. "Oh, well, yes, he did. I thought you'd come about my report."

"Report?"

"The one I made to the police. We've been looking for him as well. We've been really worried. It's not like him at all, just to disappear like that. I only left it a couple of days before reporting it."

"I see. And when was that?"

"He worked on the last day of the month but didn't turn up on the first. Left us a bit in the lurch, it's the start of our busy period."

"We're not actually here about his disappearance, but a cousin of his, Johan Christiansen."

Dag turned to Martin who showed the woman the photo of Johan.

"Perhaps you may have seen him. About the time Jørgen went missing would be a guess."

She took a good look at it. "Yes," she said, "I'm sure that's him. He came asking for Jørgen a couple of days beforehand. He shared Jørgen's room for a night or two. Not supposed to really, of course, but he had nowhere to stay so I turned a blind eye."

"Jørgen's room? Where would that be?"

"Here at the hotel. We've got a number of room for staff, there's not enough locally, if we didn't we wouldn't get anyone to work here."

""Do you think it would be possible to take a look at it? It might give us some clues. Hopefully we'll be able to find both of them and clear the whole thing up for you."

"Yes, certainly, no-one's been in there since. I've just been hoping he'll turn up again."

She turned and called through to a rear office and asked another young woman for the keys who brought them out.

"Ingrid, can you show the policemen to Jørgen's room?"

It was a basic room. A single bed, a wardrobe with a suitcase on top of it, bedside table, computer desk and a couple of chairs. On one wall was a bookcase with a dozen books on it, mostly science fiction and fantasy novels by the looks of them. On the bedside table were two used coffee mugs. A kettle stood on the floor and a milk carton was on the window sill from which the sour smell of old milk emanated. A duvet lay on the floor, probably used by Johan. Beside it were some tourist information pamphlets.

Ingrid excused herself and asked that they bring the key back to her when they'd finished which they promised they would.

Dag turned to the wardrobe and looked inside. There were still clothes and other items inside. Jørgen had not packed everything when he'd left which might suggest he was in a particular hurry or he had every intention of returning. The suitcase on top of it was empty.

Martin checked out the bedside table, a drawer in the computer desk and under the bed. There was nothing unusual; the two magazines he found under the bed were not surprising for any young man to have around.

Dag took a look at the pamphlets.

"Johan seemed interested in the local area. They may not have gone too far. Jørgen would know the area well if he's been working here for a while. Perhaps he knew of somewhere safe to hide out."

"I wonder if the hotel's had any other unusual guests?" Martin thought out loud.

"Good point. Let's go back to reception."

The woman who they'd spoken to was the manageress rather than just a receptionist and was able to give them a printout of the guests they'd had at the time of Johan and Jørgen's disappearance. The majority were couples and mostly belonged to two groups of tourists who had arrived by coach. There were only two single people who'd booked in; one a women whom the Manageress remembered as being in her fifties, and the other a man she believed was in his mid thirties who had told her he was there on business and had only stayed for one night, the night before the disappearance. She couldn't remember if he's arrived by car or train, but he had booked in quite late on, at about eight in the evening. If he'd come by train it would have been the last one in that day.

Dag asked her for a more detailed description but she could only say that he had dark hair, was of average height, and dressed in a very ordinary way. She had hardly taken much notice of him and nothing stood out about him that would make her particularly recognise him again.

"What was his name?"

She looked at the list. "He booked in as Patrik Sandberg. He was Swedish."

Dag nodded as Martin made a note of the name.

"Did Jørgen have any close or special friends here at the hotel or in Flåm, a girlfriend perhaps?"

"I don't think he had a regular girlfriend. He was friendly with Ingrid and the other girls. If he went out he would have gone with our sous chef, Eirik, they were more like best friends."

"Perhaps Eirik may be able to help?"

"He will have just gone off shift now lunch is over, I'll see if he's about."

She headed off to the kitchens after first asking Ingrid to look after reception.

Dag took the opportunity to talk to her. "Were you friends with Jørgen?" he asked.

"Yes, we were friends, he was nice. But just friends, nothing else."

"You must be worried about him; disappearing like this?"

"Well, everyone's concerned; it's just not like him." She said a little nervously.

"What about his visitor, his cousin, did you meet him?"

"Yes Jørgen introduced us. I was on duty when he arrived here."

"What was he like? I mean did he seem anxious or nervous in any way? Or was he relaxed?"

Ingrid took a moment to think. "Well, he did seem a little nervous, yes. Jørgen was working but came out to see him. They went off along the corridor towards the kitchen and talked for a while before the chef called Jørgen back to work. Jørgen gave him the key to his room and told him to wait there. He asked me not to say anything Elise; that's the mangers name. But she found out in the morning."

"Did you see them after that?"

Before she could answer Elise came back. With her was the sous chef Eirik.

"Maybe we could talk again later." Dag suggested to Ingrid.

Elise gave a rather icy stare and Ingrid returned to the office.

"This is Eirik." She said.

"Could we go somewhere quiet to talk?" Dag asked.

"There's a small room over there to by the entrance to the restaurant Elise pointed out.

"Good. Came on Eirik let's have a chat."

Eirik was 19, blond haired and blue eyed.

"So," Dag said looking directly into Eirik's eyes,"Eirik what do you know about Jørgen's disappearance?"

"Me? Why should I know anything?"

Dag could tell right away that Eirik knew something. The young man's fair face blushed a pink hue almost before speaking.

"People are worried about him, and his cousin. You met his cousin Johan." Dag made it a statement rather than a question.

"Eirik nervously held his right hand with his left on his lap. "Yea, I met him. We had a beer in his room after I finished work."

"What did you talk about?"

Eirik shrugged. "Just talked."

Dag smiled. "Come on Eirik, you can do better than that. You must have asked what Johan was doing here, why he had come, what he was up to? You did didn't you. You hardly talked about the weather."

"He was in some sort of trouble. I could tell. Didn't say what. Said he had to get away. It was the only place he could think of coming. He didn't want to found, he said. Wanted to hide out."

Dag nodded. "But he couldn't hide out here, not in this or hotel or even in Flåm?"

"He wanted to know if we knew anywhere he could stay. Jørgen said he may know somewhere, or knew someone who could help. But they didn't tell me!"

"Who else could he have talked to? Any ideas who he might have known that could have helped?"

Eirik shrugged again. "There's Ingrid. And he knew one of the barmen at the Cockerel Microbrewery quite well, don't know which one though."

"Very well, Eirik, that'll be all for now, thanks for your help."

They went back to reception. Elise was still at the desk.

"Could we have just one final word with Ingrid?"

Elise sighed. "We are just about to receive a whole coach-load of tourists."

Dag smiled. "It won't take long, just a quick word. It would be better to get it all over and done with now rather than have to came back and start all over again."

"Very well. Ingrid!" she called.

Ingrid came out again and Dag took her to a quiet corner of the reception area.

"Are you sure Jørgen told you nothing about what he was up to or thinking of? May his cousin told you something?"

She shook her head. "No he didn't. We would often talk, about all sorts. We used to tell each other everything. But he wouldn't tell me. I knew something was wrong as soon as his cousin turned up. He was only a second cousin though, I think. They hardly knew each other really. I don't know how he made him do it. But I'm sure it was his fault."

"Hmm, he knew someone at the bar in town? Any idea who?"

She shook her head again. He'd go there sometimes, but it's expensive, I didn't go."

"OK Ingrid, thanks for telling us. Don't worry, we'll find him, they're probably shacked up in some mountain cabin somewhere having a great time."

"The microbrewery boss?"

"Sounds a good idea. For more than one reason. Hopefully they food as well as drink. We'll need to get to that hostel soon or we might lose our beds."

"I'll call them; confirm we're definitely on the way."

They were both still carrying holdalls with the few things they need for a couple of days on the road but it was only a short walk to the bar. On the way they passed the railway station and a small selection of shops.

"Boss." Martin said quietly as he walked close to Dag. "We've just passed the station. I only had a glance but could, have sworn I got a glimpse of someone ducking into the clothes shop on the corner. A man; looked rather familiar."

"Well don't look back. Take no notice. But we'll have to keep our eyes peeled if he's back on our track."

The bar was quiet. There was just the one barman working and a couple of table with a few tourists by the look of them. It was not the time of day for local custom, if they relied much on it anyway.

"Let's just get a beer and something to eat first; that's if they're still serving food" Dag said as they walked to the bar. It was wooden, solid and had furniture carved from the trunks of trees as well as leather sofas, with a semi circular curved bar near the entrance. Even though the weather was mild it had an open wood burner blazing in the centre of the room with a three quarter circle of built in benches around it.

They ordered their beers and the barman had to go and check if the cook was still there. He returned, and luckily he was. They settled for simple bacon burgers with deep fried potatoes and mayo. And took a seating area against a wall in the centre of the room where they could have a good view of everything including the door.

Whilst waiting for their food Dag sent a text to Rolf to keep him up to date then phoned the Chief. The call was quite brief.

"That didn't take long." Martin commented.

"He was remarkably quiet if not relaxed. Just said that, as our investigation was authorised at the highest level, he could hardly interfere. I think he meant that he was able and happy to keep out of it and if anything went wrong it would not be his responsibility."

"That's a relief."

"For him, yes."

Dag's phone buzzed. It was a text from Rolf. He thanked him for the update and wrote just three more words, 'support at hand'.

Dag showed it to Martin.

"Have they got someone on the ground here already?"

"Seems like it."

"Maybe it's our stalker."

Dag shook his head. "He was there in Bergen. That was too soon. No, he's not E14 that's for sure."

Their meal came and they took time to eat and drink. By the time they'd finished the tourists had wanders off and they were the only customers.

"Come on; let's have a talk with the barman."

Dag showed the barman his ID. "Could we just have a quick word?"

The barman looked around.

"You've no other customers; you can talk to us at the bar. You know Jørgen Arnesen; he works at the Aurlands Hotel." Dag made it a statement, the barman was bound to know him.

"Jørgen? What's happened to him? I heard he's gone missing."

"I was told the barman here was a good friend of his, would that be you?"

"Not me, I usually do the day shift, if came in it would normally be late at night when he finished work. He'd talk to Sigurd, Sigurd Eriksen, he was more of a friend."

"Is eh around?"

"He'll back on at ....." the barman looked at the clock, "...six"

"There's someone else we're trying to locate as well."

Martin produced the photo of Johan. And showed it to him.

"Have you seen this man at all?"

The barman took a good look. "No, I've not seen him. Mind you we get lots of tourists here I don't take that much notice of them all."

"Very well. If you see Sigurd let him know we'll be around this evening for a word. Martin, let's go and sort out our accommodation."

As they reached the door it opened almost banging in to Dag so that he had to take a step back.

A tall blond woman almost burst through. She raised a pair of sunglasses she was wearing and shook her long hair.

Oh, I'm so sorry! Couldn't see a thing through these, it's dark in here."

She gave Dag and then Martin a big smile. Perfect white teeth flashed at them. She looked young but Dag thought that is was the fact that her almost perfect skin made her look so. Martin appraised the rest of her body enveloped in a tight fitting black dress which emphasised a figure that may not have been very youthful but gave every indication that it was well cared for. She could have been taken for a number of years younger than perhaps she was. On her shoulder she carried a large red sports bag, big enough to hold any necessities for a weekend away. She sauntered over to the bar and, after another moment watching her Dag and Martin resumed their exit.

"Well that cheered me up!" Martin said brightly. "I wonder where's she staying, maybe she'll still be there when we come back."

Dag gave a laugh. "Hoping against hope there Martin, way out of your league."

"Oh, I can turn it on when I want to. Anyway who's to say what her tastes are?"

"An older man perhaps?"

"I wouldn't let the wife hear you say that!"

There was a taxi at the station and it only took them five minutes to get to the hostel. It was made up of three large houses linked together set in farmland by the banks of a river with rocky mountain slopes rising to the other side with cataracts of water rushing down their sides at several places. The rooms were basic but comfortable, the bathrooms were clean, although they had to decide on who would get the upper or lower bunk bed, they had good wifi and kitchen facilities for self-catering; not that Dag and Martin had thought of buying any supplies.

When they had settled in, showered and changed they decided to walk back into the town. It had only taken five minutes in the taxi so shouldn't take them more than twenty minutes to walk it. They would be there in plenty of time to question Sigurd. And Martin mused that the woman might still be there. Dag just gave another laugh but said nothing.

They passed the Aurlands Hotel again on the way back. Two large coaches no stood in their car park.

Dag glanced over the hotel frontage. His eye caught a movement in one of the bedroom windows; the curtains had made a sudden movement. He shook his head. He was getting jumpy. Why wouldn't any of the guests be looking out of a window at the scenery? It was just that the very brief sight he got of the figure was what made him nervous. It looked like the figure of a man, but only a, and maybe just his imagination. But for some reason his intuition as telling him that that it was what he saw and that he'd seen that figure before, or was his judgement playing tricks on him?

Then just as they'd passed the hotel a taxi pulled up in the car park. Both Martin and Dag looked back. From out of the car came the tall blond woman from the Cockerel. The driver leapt out, took her bag from the boot and passed it to her. She paid him and set off into the hotel. As she reached the door she turned. Dag had turned away but Martin still watched her. As she sent through the door she hesitated for just a second and, briefly, Martin thought, flashed him a modest smile.

"Well now, I wonder if she'll go back to the Cockerel tonight?" Martin pondered.

"You still hoping?"

"She smiled at me, I'm sure she did."

Dag nodded. "I suppose she could have found you amusing."

Martin shook his head. "You wait and see; that's all."

"Come on, we're here to see this Sigurd guy." Dag sighed.

Sigurd was there ready to start his shift, but he had fifteen minutes to spare so they could take him to one side and question him without it interfering with his work.

"You were friends with Jørgen Arnesen." Dag stated.

"We used to talk, yes. We weren't all that close though."

"What did you used to talk about?"

"Books. We read the same ones. And war-gaming. We both played the same one; War of Clans. He was Faceless, I was Hawk."

"Hmm. How did he play it, did he have a computer?"

"A laptop, yes."

"When did you last see him?"

"The 31st. They say he disappeared the next day."

"And you've not heard from him at all?" Martin intervened.

"No, nothing."

"He had a mobile phone, though, I suppose. Did you have his number?" Dag asked him.

"Yes he had a mobile. And no I've not heard from him. I tried calling but it's either switched off or there's no signal."

Martin asked the next question. "Was there anyone with him when you last saw him?"

"Yes, a cousin of his, Johan I think his name was."

"Is this him?" Martin asked showing him Johan's photo.

"Yes that's him."

"So, what else did you talk about that night? Not just books and war-gaming I imagine." Dag continued.

Sigurd looked from one to the other. He was considering what to say.

"Don't try hiding anything, if you want we can always take a long trip to a station and do a full interview. It could take several days. You wouldn't want that now would you?" Dag told him.

Sigurd left a breath out. "It was something to do with his cousin. In was in some sort of trouble. They didn't tell me what. But they wanted to find somewhere he could hide out, keep out of the way for a while. I didn't think Jørgen would go with him."

"And where did they go?"

Sigurd shook his head again. "I don't know, they'd gone the next day. I said I'd try and think of a place. There's cabins up in the mountains around here, trekkers use them they used to be used by hunters. I was going to ask around, but as I said they 'd gone off themselves."

"And who else around here knows these cabins? Who would you have asked?"

"My uncle, he goes out hunting, he knows them all well."

"And where can we find your uncle?"

"Here. He owns the place. He should be in soon."

Dag thanked him and let him go to work. Martin ordered two more drinks whilst they waited for his uncle. They had sat in the same seating as before. It wasn't long before people started arriving; it was that time of day, tourists had completed their tours and locals were finishing work. They watched each of the newcomers. One man came in alone and talked immediately to Sigurd who nodded over to them. They man looked at them, nodded to Sigurd and came over.

He held out his hand. "Theo, Theo Osen."

"Please sit down Mr Osen. Just a few questions, won't take long." Dag replied. "Sigurd told us that you talked to Jørgen Arnesen before he disappeared; and his cousin as well."

"Yes, it must have been the night before."

Dag gave him a quizzical look waiting for him to elaborate.

Theo hesitated then continued. "It seemed that Jørgen's cousin was in some sort of trouble, back in Bergen I think he said. Owed someone money and they were after him; not nice people he said. They wanted to know is there was somewhere safe to hide out for a while until things settled down and he was sure the moneylenders hadn't followed him here. A foreign gang I shouldn't wonder."

"And what did you suggest?" Did you know anywhere they could use?"

"There're a few places, but it would be best to take a guide. They're not so easy to find. I told them I'd think about it and see them the next day. But then they didn't come back, they scarpered anyway. Maybe the gang turned up and frightened them off."

"Was there anything else they said that might have suggested what they thought of doing?"

Theo shook his head. "Don't think so."

"Well, have a think. And if you remember anything let us know. We're staying at the hostel just outside of Flåm

"OK, if can think of anything I'll let you know." He stood up to go back to the bar. "Oh, actually, there was something his cousin said; what was it now?" He stood and thought. "They were at the bar and his cousin had a text on his phone. He said something like 'it's from him, we've got to go'. That's about it."

Dag nodded. "Well, thanks, if there's anything else..."

"Sure." And Theo head off.

"So," said Martin, "Johan still had his phone and he's getting texts from someone. I though his phone wasn't working."

"A new phone probably, pay-as-you-go probably. They're cheap enough and pretty well untraceable."

"And someone's in contact with him?"

"And I wonder who that someone is? Whoever it is they're gave him a warning."

The door swung open.

In strode the woman. She had changed her dress. Now she was clothed in an equally hugging red number with a black silken shawl draped over her shoulders.

"Well now, as I hoped, things are looking up." Martins smiled as he downed his drink. "Want another?" He asked Dag.

"Just one more perhaps; someone needs to keep an eye on you."

The woman had ordered a large gin and tonic. Martin managed to get next to her to order his own drinks. But she had started a conversation with Theo who'd been more than quick enough to serve her, but she was turned away from Martin. He was hoping that there might be a gap in their conversation so he could talk to her and introduce himself. But she took no notice of him and talked and laughed with Theo. He had to return to the table without success.

Dag smiled. "Losing you touch?"

"There's time yet."

"If you're going to make a night of it, I'll leave you to it. I'm off after this." He said raising his glass. "Just don't wake me up and trample on top of me when you get back."

9.

Dag woke as the sun broke through a gap in the curtains. He looked at his watch. It was just before seven. He yawned and stretched.

'At least,' he thought, 'he wasn't woken by Martin coming in during the night.'

He pulled off the duvet and eased himself off the lower bunk. He turned with his head at the same height as the upper bunk. It was empty. Martin was not there. Dag had not been woken by him because he hadn't returned.

Dag gave a grunt. So, Martin seemed to have been lucky after all. He couldn't help feeling a slight pang of envy. It must have been that woman. Martin would have enjoyed the luxury of her hotel room as well as her bed last night, he imagined. Well, as long as he was available for duty on time; he'd leave it a while and him a wake-up call at 08.30 if he hadn't returned. For now he'd shower, dress and see what breakfast was available. He was dying for a good, hot, strong coffee. He didn't drink much at all these days and the few beers last night had been strong and he was feeling their effect.

He had two large mugs of coffee in the kitchen area whilst checking his phone. There were no messages and there'd been no calls during the night. Another guest offered him some croissants but he thanked him and refused; his stomach didn't feel up to it. He watched the news on the wall mounted TV and then checked his watch. It was 08.20. He decided to give Martin a call.

Martin's phone didn't ring. Dag sighed. It annoyed him. Had Martin turned it off or wasn't it charged. He would wait another twenty minutes or so in the hope that he'd turn up.

Twenty minutes passed and there was still no sign of Martin.

There was nothing for it Dag would have to go to the hotel.

At 08.35 he set off and was at the hotel fifteen minutes later. He went to the reception desk, but wondered what to say, how put it to the receptionist. It was a different girl than before. He decided it was best not to ask directly for Martin.

"Good morning." He greeted her, showing his ID. "I wonder if you could help me. I need to speak to a lady staying at the hotel."

He explained that he didn't know her name and so described her.

The receptionist knew immediately who he meant. She also remembered her name; Rita Hustad.

"But," said the girl, "she's already booked out, before breakfast. She got a taxi, maybe she went to the station. There's a train just left; 08.35."

Dag frowned. "It's an awkward question but did she have any visitors last night that you are aware of?"

The girl gave a grin. "I wouldn't know, Sir, I only came on at eight and I only saw her on her own."

"In that case would it be possible to see her room? I'm sure your manager Elise wouldn't mind she let me in to Jørgen's room yesterday. I'm really here trying to find him, but I need to find out about this woman as well. So, if you'd be able to give me the keys now that she's gone, I'd be very grateful."

She hesitated. "Elise isn't here this morning."

"WE had a long chat yesterday. She said she'd do anything to help me find Jørgen. I'm sure you'd want the same."

"Well, I suppose so." She turned to the key cupboard and took out a set of room keys. "There it's room 203 on the second floor."

"Thank you, that's most helpful. I'll only be a few minutes, just a quick check."

He turned the key in the lock as quietly and carefully as he could and eased the door open. He looked inside. To the right was a bathroom and ahead he could see into one part of the room. To the right, and out of view must have been the bed. Large windows let in the bright sunlight. One of the windows had been left ajar and a light breeze blew through it making the curtains flutter. All was quite.

He stepped softly inside and walked slowly passed the bathroom and into the bedroom. Everything was neat and tidy. The bed was empty and looked as if it had been made. There was nothing out of place. He should have asked if the cleaners had already been in.

He looked into the built-in wardrobe. All that was in it were some spare pillows and duvet.

He turned back to the bathroom and went in. Again it looked tidy and almost unused. But here he could smell the recently used washing scents and cosmetics. It was the only sign that the woman had stayed there.

There was no sign of Martin or that he'd been there. Dag was now becoming concerned.

He went back down to reception. Ingrid was with the new girl.

Dag passed the keys back to the girl and thanked her.

"Ingrid. Good morning. We're still working on the case; found out a few things yesterday. I'm sure we're making progress. Hopefully we'll find Jørgen and his cousin soon. Tell me, have you seen my colleague about. He had a few things to attend to and I seem to have mislaid him?"

"No Sir I've not seen him."

"Oh. Were you on duty last night?"

"Yes, till twelve, then the night porter came on."

"I was just wondering if you saw one of your guests, Ms Rita Hustad, I believe her name is, return last night?"

"Not whilst I was on duty, no." She paused. "I think she must have come back later, I'm sure her key was still in the cupboard when I left, I usually check to see if anyone is still out and mention it to the porter."

"I see, thank you. What time does the Cockerel open?"

"Not till midday."

"The man who owns it, Theo Osen, do you know where he lives?"

The two girls looked at each other. The second one spoke. "He lives in the bright yellow coloured farmhouse just off the Nedre Brekkevegen on this side of the river. There's a track that leads to it; it's one of a group of houses. You can't miss it."

"Thank you again, you've been a great help." He smiled, turned and walked out. He couldn't help but get a quick glimpse of the two girls giving each other an odd look.

Once outside he tried again to call Martin but still there was silence.

He looked at the map on his phone as he had no paper one. He wished he'd stopped off at the tourist information office to get one. He found the road and the group of farm houses and set off.

He had to go passed the station again and decided to take a quick look around. The place was quiet. He noticed that the next train was due to leave shortly at 09.45. On his way out he went to the ticket office, showed his ID and asked the clerk if he's seen the woman that morning. He said not.

Attached to the station was the tourist information office. Dag took both the opportunity to get a map of the area and a few pamphlets and also to ask the staff there if they had seen her. Again it was negative.

He took the main road over the river bridge and just along from the junction on the opposite bank he could see the track leading to the group of farmhouses including one painted bright yellow.

It only took a few minutes to get to the front door. He knocked loudly. At first there was no sound so he knocked louder still. Then there was the sound of movement inside. There was the muffled sound of complaint and then the door unlocked and opened.

A ruffled and dressing-gowned Theo stood in the doorway.

"What the hell do you want?"

"To talk to you Mr Osen. Would you prefer we did here on the doorstep? Or perhaps you'd prefer to invite me in and not give the neighbours anything to talk about."

Theo groaned and his shoulders slumped. "Come in I'll get some coffee on. That's what you'll expect I suppose."

"Very kind of you Mr Osen don't mind if I do. But I don't way to keep you for long, and matters are getting a bit more urgent."

"You've heard something?" Theo asked as they came into the kitchen. "Take a seat."

Dag sat at the kitchen table.

"I've not heard much more concerning Jørgen and his cousin, no. I was hoping you may have had time to think about things. But something else has cropped up and I need to ask you some other questions. It's concerning a customer of yours last night."

Theo passed him a mug of coffee. He'd only made instant. Dag had hoped for fresh. But it was coffee.

"Customer?"

"Yes that rather attractive woman in the red dress. You seemed to be getting on well before I left."

Theo brightened and smiled. "Ah, yes her." Then his smile left him. "We were getting on great until your mate put his oar in."

"Oh yes, tell me."

He shrugged. "Started chatting her up, Bought drinks and they went and sat down; a nice quiet corner. It got busy after that."

"So did you see them leave?"

He shook his head. "As I said it got busy and anyway I had to go into the office and do some paperwork. When I came back they'd gone."

"About how long would that have been?"

"No more than half an hour. Wouldn't have been much later than ten."

"Which barman was on?"

"Two of them, Sigurd and Sven."

"Will they be on duty today?"

"They should both be in now." Theo said looking at his watch. "They should be doing a stock check."

"Then I'll go and have a word with them." Dag said standing. He put down the coffee mug. "Thanks for the coffee. If I've got any more questions I'll be back."

Theo scowled at Dag's back as he walked away and closed the front door behind him.

As he walked back across the bridge towards the Cockerel he phoned the hostel and asked them to check if Martin had returned. By the time he'd reached the Cockerel they had called back to say there was no sign of him.

He banged loudly on the front door of the bar. He could see the barmen inside. It was Sigurd who came to the door.

"A quick word if I may?" Dag asked him.

Sigurd moved away from the door and let him in.

"With both of you actually."

"Both of us?"

Dag walked to the bar where Sven was counting bottles behind the bar. Sigurd joined him.

"Last night," Dag continued, "I left my associate here having a drink."

"Oh him, yes." Sigurd nodded.

"What did he do after I left?"

Sigurd smiled. "He came up to the bar when Theo had to go to the office. Ordered some drinks for himself and that woman. Chatted her up. I could see he was going to do that even when he was sat with you."

"And then?"

"That sat over there." Sigurd said, pointing to a table at the back of the room. He bought two more rounds and her drinks weren't cheap. Not that it did him much good."

"What do you mean?"

"She left without him"

"They didn't leave together?"

"No, as I said she left on her own. It wasn't too late, towards half eleven I suppose."

"And what did my associate do then?"

"Came back and sat at the bar." Sigurd looked over at Sven.

Sven spoke with a grin. "Didn't seem very happy. She dumped him I guess, just led him on."

"And then? Did he stay or go? You're making this hard work for me."

Sigurd answered. "He drank his bottle of beer and left."

"Almost banged it down on the table." Sven added.

"And that's it, he just left. When would that be – before twelve?"

"Just, yes."

"Did you notice anything else? Any strangers, anyone acting strangely? Anything unusual at all?"

Sigurd shook his head. "Half the people in were tourists. Strangers to us. Can't think of anything unusual, he just upped and left."

Dag sighed. "Very well. If you think of anything let me know." And he turned to leave.

"Oh," said Sven, "I did notice a guy leave just after him"

Dag turned back. "Tell me."

Sven gave a slight shrug. "He was drinking on his own I think, not with any group. Sat over there by the window. Didn't take much notice of him really. Only has the one drink as far as I can remember."

"Can you describe him?"

Sven's brow creased and he stared at the ceiling. "Not really. I didn't take much notice. Just an ordinary guy. Average height. Dark hair I think. I really can't be sure. But I just happen to see him leave right after your mate."

Dag thanked him and left the bar. He stood outside thinking.

The woman and the man. Who were they? What were they doing here? He could guess what the man was up to, it must be their stalker. But the woman; what was she in all this, if anything? And where the hell was Martin, what had happened to him?

His concern was turning into anxiety. He called the hostel again and asked them to check. But he guessed what their answer would be.

He needed a decent coffee.

Sat at a cafe table he updated Rolf by text and made sure he was aware of his concerns. He put off calling the Chief; he could do without any distress from him for now. He'd leave it until he got some sort of answer. But where to find an answer? He sat staring into his coffee. He felt he was at a dead end. Where could he go next? He tried think of any other leads.

All he could think to do was to retrace Martins footsteps, or what they should have been, back to the hostel from the bar. Or perhaps he'd got a taxi. That was the next stop, the taxi rank at the station.

As he arrived there his phone rang. It was Rolf. He had phone not texted this time.

He too was concerned. Was Dag sure that the man was the same as the one in Bergen. Dag couldn't be sure, but who else could it be? Had he heard yet from Martin, was there any sign of him? Dag said no. And did he have a name for the woman? Dag told him - Rita Hustad.

"You said that Martin spoke to her in the bar?"

"Yes."

"And he disappeared afterward?"

"That's what I was told."

"And you don't think that Johan and his cousin set off for a cabin?"

"They could have. The bar owner that they'd talked to, that had knowledge of the cabins, said he thought not, They'd have need a guide to be sure of finding one."

"For now I can only suggest that you do all you can to find Martin. It might lead us to Johan. And, as I said before, we do have support close by. But there are reasons that I can tell you no more. You'll have to trust me."

'Not a lot of help.' thought Dag after the call ended. 'Basically I'm back where I was – on my own.'

There was one taxi parked up. Dag asked the driver if he'd been on shift the night before. But this driver only worked during the day, he left his son to do the night shift. He'd wouldn't be starting work until six that evening. Dag, after again displaying his ID, asked where he lived as he needed to speak to him urgently. The driver told him that he wouldn't like being woken up in the middle of the day. Dag asked him if he would prefer to go to a police station kilometres away. The driver grudgingly offered to take him to his house.

His son could not remember picking up Martin, but he did take the woman back to her hotel.

Dag thought of the hotel. He had been stupid. He had been concentrating on the woman when they checked her room. He had not thought of checking on the mystery man.

The taxi driver was kind enough to drive him the short distance there.

He looked up at the hotel trying to remember from which room he saw the curtains move. He was sure it was on the second floor towards the left side. In fact, it would have been close to the woman's room, if not next door.

He was back in reception.

"Me again, I'm afraid." He told the new girl. "I've got one more favour to ask."

Ingrid had seen him from the open door of the office and came out as well.

"There was a man staying here, on his own I would think, would have had a room close to Rita Hustad. He probably arrived a couple of days before. I wondered if I could have a look at the bookings."

"If you'd like to come to the office?" Ingrid suggested.

Dag smiled. She would prefer he wasn't repeatedly at the reception desk, or perhaps she would prefer he talk to her away from the other girl.

He went around the desk and into the office. She closed the door.

"Have you heard anything yet?" She asked him.

"About Jørgen and Johan? No nothing else I'm afraid. But I've got something more important to deal with for now. Do you have the booking?"

"Yes, of course. It's just that I remembered something his cousin said."

Dag showed interest. "Which was?"

"I heard him say to Jørgen something like 'we've got to hide the computer, don't let him get it'."

"Hmm, I see." Dag nodded. "That might be useful. Now, the bookings?"

She opened a window on her computer. "You might as well look at it on here."

"Thanks." He scrolled through the bookings forms. He stopped. It was a booking for room 205, just two doors away from Rita. The name was Jan Haaland. He remembered it. It was the name used by the man who got into the Police Station and stole the memory stick.

"Who's this, do you remember him?"

"She looked at the name. "Um, yes, I think so. He was on his own. Can't say I saw him much, maybe only the once, but I may not have been on duty when he was around. He booked out then." She said pointed to a date and time.

He had booked out just fifteen minutes after Rita. But Dag remembered that the manageress and told him of another man, in his thirties, who'd been there before for just and had booked out the day before the boys' disappearance. Was it the same man? He certainly hadn't used the same name; the previous man was called Patrik Sandberg and was supposed to be Swedish. But, although both descriptions were vague Dag had the feeling that he was one and the same.

He thought of having a look at the room but realised it would yield nothing. It would have been cleaned and reused probably since his departure.

What he must do was get back to the question of finding Martin. As the minutes and hours ticked by it would become more and more urgent.

10.

Martin came awake. His head pounded. He remembered drinking and he remembered the woman. He hadn't thought the beer had been that strong.

He moved, or at least attempted to. He tried to open his eyes but couldn't. He groaned, but the sound did not come from his mouth.

He was lying on his side his hands held out in front of him. He pulled his arms towards him but they refused to move. He was tied up against something solid. He felt the tight blindfold that had been put around his eyes. And he felt what was stuck to his mouth to prevent him opening it.

He pulled his legs towards his body. They too had been secured around the ankles.

He took a few deep breaths trying to clear his head. It wasn't just the beer that was causing his discomfort. Now he could feel where the pain was worst. He could sense the lump on his head without being able to put his hand to it. He had been knocked out and taken somewhere; held somewhere.

He had two senses he could still use. He listened. It was almost eerily quite. He though he heard the sound of a bird singing in the distance but that was all. He took another breath and smelled the air. There was mustiness to it, but not an indoor one. There was the smell of wood and, he was sure, of straw or hay. The faint smell of animals that might once have used the place. He was in a barn or farm building, he was certain of it.

His head throbbed. The pain of it went through to his eyes and the back of his neck. His mouth was bone dry and he was desperate for a drink.

He pulled himself up against what was a large pillar or column that he was tied to and tried to relax. He wondered how long he had been there and what time of day it was. It must be morning but he had no real way of knowing.

For a moment he though he heard the far off noise of a vehicle, maybe a tractor but within seconds the sound had faded away. Then he thought the call of a cow wafted through the air but still too distant to be sure.

He pulled and tugged at his wrist bindings. Then he raised his legs towards his hands to check what secured his legs. They were not ropes but a metal band held firmly with a lock of some sort; there was no way he could loosen it with his hands. He let his legs drop back down again. If he tried too hard he would merely damage his wrists and his ankles.

There was little for it but to wait and see what happened.

He only hoped that someone would return that he wouldn't be left there unable to call for help and without any water. A man can survive for ages without food, but not without water. And with his head feeling as it did and his mouth so parched already he didn't relish a long wait.

He thought back to the bar the previous evening.

He had believed he'd got on well with Rita. They'd drank and talked. He remembered the touch of her leg against his under the table. He recalled the strong scent she was wearing. He could see again her lips as they smiled and the sparkle in her blue eyes. He believed she really like him, she fancied him, that his night would be very different to what had evidently had come to pass. He still couldn't understand why she had left so abruptly. She said she had to go and powder her nose; an old fashioned expression. And when she came back she simply said that she had to go, thanked him for the drinks and left; all in a very offhand manner. Something had happened when she'd gone to the toilet, something that had changed her attitude to him.

And then he was left alone at the bar.

He didn't stay. He remembered that. He had decided to walk back to the hostel. Get some fresh air. And it was the fresh air that hit him as soon as he was outside; more than it usually would. He remembered starting to walk. He didn't think he'd gone far but the memory of it was a blur. He remembered haziness, and was it dizziness? Then everything went black.

He couldn't remember anything more until he woke here. He wondered if he could get to his phone, it had been in his back pocket. He wriggled about. He could tell it wasn't there. It had been taken, and so had his wallet which had been in the other back pocket. He could feel they were both empty.

He was hot. The time passed. He felt a beam of sunlight hit his cheek and he was feeling sleepy. His head was hurting a little less now but he was desperate for something to drink. He felt his head sag. He quickly brought it upright. But it sagged again once, then twice. He dozed off.

He woke again suddenly. There had been a noise. He was immediately alert.

Yes, he heard it now. It sounded like a door had been opened and was closing. There was movement. The sound of footsteps came towards him. He tried to speak but only a muffled moan came from his sealed lips. The steps came close and then circled to his rear. He sensed the presence of someone standing behind him.

Something touched his hands. He was just able to grasp it. It was a bottle, a plastic one. Hands came from behind him, grasped the tape and tore it off. He couldn't help but yelp when it ripped off. He gulped in a lungful through his mouth. He tried to talk but his mouth was so dry nothing but croak came out. A hand pulled his hands and the bottle towards his lips. He felt the hand and it made him shudder at first and then realised that whoever it was wore gloves of some sort.

The bottle came to his lips. There was no cap on it and he could hold back his head and greedily drink down the water. He tried not to drink it all. It may be all he would get and it was never a good idea to drink too much at once.

He took a few more breaths and tried to speak again. This time words came out.

"Who are you? Why have you done this?"

There was no reply.

"Talk to me. How can I be of use to you if you don't talk to me? What is it you want?"

There was still silence. Then a sound of what Martin thought was tape being pulled from a roll. He was right. In a flash tape was wrapped around his mouth again. He tried to keep his mouth open but his chin was grabbed and pulled up and the tape secured before he had time to react.

He shouted but was left with nothing but an incoherent moan reached his ears. The only other sound were of the footsteps moving away from him and then the door being opened and shut.

He was alone again.

*

In the hostel kitchen, with a strong coffee before him, Dag sat and thought. He'd walked the route between the Cockerel and the hostel. Nothing stood out as a clue.

Martin's laptop was on his bunk. Dag looked at it. The laptop held the memory stick data, the thing that this was all about, the crux of it all other than what Johan may know or have. What Ingrid had told him about Johan and Jørgen hiding a computer led him to believe that Johan also may have kept a copy. Did someone have a suspicion that Martin and he had done the same? Was that why Martin had disappeared, or perhaps been abducted? Could Johan and Jørgen also have been abducted or had they managed to get away? If Johan and Jørgen had found it necessary to hide theirs he had better do the same; but where?

He went back to the room relieved to find that the laptop was still there.

But where to hide it?

He couldn't leave it here at the hostel. It would be no secret that they were staying here. Where could he take it? Was there anywhere safe or was there anyone trustworthy?

He could only think of one person and that was Ingrid. She already knew that Johan's computer might have some connection to Jørgen's disappearance and might even assume that Martin's was his and be willing to keep it hidden.

He went to the kitchen and found a hemp shopping bag and put the computer in it wrapped in a spare jumper to make it look as innocuous as possible. He wished he had a weapon. They were up against a person or persons who were only too willing to kill. But it was against the rules. Their heckler and Koch's were kept locked down in patrol cars. But he'd broken that rule and then he set off yet again for the hotel. And he knew that he must soon speak to the Chief and tell him the bad news.

Ingrid was just leaving after an early start. Dag caught her just as she left the hotel. He called over to her and asked to speak. He wanted to do so quietly and with her alone so they walked around to tot rear of the building and stopped by a rear entrance. There was no-one else about.

"I would like to ask a favour."

"What sort of favour?" she asked in a dubious voice.

"I need to put something in safe keeping, a computer."

"A computer?" She frowned.

"Yes, it might seem strange, but I can't keep it with me and I don't want anyone else to get their hands on it."

"Like Johan wanted Jørgen to do? What is it about these computers? What's going on?""

"That's something I'm not able to explain at the moment. For now I just have to ask you to trust me."

She looked away from him. "I'm sorry I don't want to get involved."

"Not even for Jørgen? You like him don't you. I'm trying my best to find him, and his cousin. And now my partner disappeared as well. We both have someone we need to find, and need to find them safe and sound. If you could just do this for me? You won't regret it."

She gave out a sigh, "I don't think he notices me half the time."

Dag gave a knowing smile. "I'm sure he does. You're a good looking girl. But you know what these young men are like with their computers and games; easily distracted. If he knew how you thought about him and what you're doing to help, I'm pretty sure he'd take a bit more notice."

She gave him a smile. "You're right of course, I must help. And they must be found. Ok, I'll find somewhere safe for it."

"Good, here," he said taking his jumper from the bag then passing it with the computer to her. "I don't need to know where it is just that you have safe. It's better that way. Now, let me leave first and wait a minute or two before you go. I'd sooner we weren't seen together."

With that he turned and walked back to the hotel front. As he was turning the corner of the building a taxi pulled up in the front of the hotel. He stopped and stood back peering from behind the wall. The taxi door opened and out got Rita.

She was back. But why?

*

A figure looked out from its position behind the sparse trees which lined the park on the slope to the rear of the hotel. It looked down directly onto the rear of the building and its surrounds and had a perfect view of the road at the front. The position had been easy to reach; there was a well used path which wound up from further along the road and then across the ridge of the hill. There was even a viewing point for walkers.

The figure watched the Detective meet the girl at the back of the hotel and saw him give her a bag. Then the detective left her, but as he did so a taxi arrived and that woman got out. The detective stopped and watched. Then he returned to the hotel's rear. But the figure had watched the girl. She had gone back into the hotel by a rear door. And when the detective had returned she had gone. The figure watched and saw the detective go back to the front, jump into the taxi and it drove off. All the time he had taken pictures.

The figure considered what to do. Whatever the detective had given to the girl was important, that was for sure. Perhaps he had somehow got his hands on the target's computer, but doubted it. There had been no meeting between them; unless it had been found at the address in Bergen, and that wasn't likely. This must be something else. And that woman, what was she doing back here, where had she been and gone? The figure knew that she had been in the bar the night before and had sat drinking with the other detective. For now the decision was to follow the receptionist. She may have the answer to those questions.

*

Dag Turned back and retraced his steps to speak to Ingrid. He turned the corner to where they had been talking. She had gone. Perhaps she'd gone around the building the other way or had slipped indoors.

Maybe she would leave by the front door.

He went back round to the front. The taxi driver had helped Rita in with a bag and was just about to set off in his car. Dag ran forward and stopped him in time and jumped into the back seat.

The taxi driver looked around in surprise.

"Oh, you again."

"Yes, me again. If you wouldn't mind taking me to the station; and on the way answer a few more questions."

"More? What else can I tell you?"

"The woman you've just taken to the hotel? Where did you pick her up?"

Dag could see the driver looked looking in his mirror at him. Their eyes locked. "At the station." He said.

Dag looked at his watch. The time was getting on, it was now 12.30. Did she have time to get a train somewhere and return? He thought only Myrdal would be possible but needed to check the times at the station.

The driver dropped him off without a word.

A quick check of the timetable showed that she could have gone to Myrdal and back. The early train she had taken would have got there at 09.32. There was a train back at 11.00 which arrived at 11.57 and then she got the taxi to the hotel.

What had she done in Myrdal? Or whom had she met? And why return to Flåm?

He went to the station cafe and ordered another coffee. He took out his phone, looked at it for a moment, and then dialled the Chief. He couldn't put it off any longer.

He explained everything to him. He listened silently as the Chief answered back. He held the phone a centimetre away from his ear. Anyone close by could have heard the tinny and loud voice of the Chief easily enough. Dag put it closer as the Chief's voice subsided. No matter what he had said the Chief had no real choice but to allow Dag to continue his investigation. He had to admit to Dag that he'd been called by the Politimester who had told him to give Dag his full support. But now Martin was missing he would be on his own and that was against any rules of the investigative process.

Dag agreed. There was only one thing for it, he told the Chief; the only other person who knew the case and understood the security implications was Jenny. She was the only officer that could assist him. She would have to take a plane and then the train to join him. If she left now she could be there the next morning.

The phone was silent for a moment. Dag could almost hear the Chief recalculating his budgets.

But he agreed. He would send Jenny on her way now.

Then Dag texted Rolf telling him of Rita Hustad and her return.

Should he go back to the hotel and interview Rita? It was the obvious thing to do; she was the last person to see Martin. But Dag hesitated. There was something that made him hold back, his intuition. He wanted to know what had gone on between Martin and Rita, if anything. But, if there was a link between her, Martin's disappearance and maybe the case itself, he didn't want to warn her off or show his hand.

What to do this afternoon. He couldn't just sit about and do nothing. Martin had to be somewhere. He had to be found. Dag could only imagine what may have happened to him and what danger he might be in. He could not forget that a man had been killed, and apparently in cold blood. Whoever was behind it would surely have no compunction at taking another life.

He shook his head. Why, if as Rolf said, there was support close by, hadn't they made themselves know and come to his aid? He could understand an agent needing to keep under cover, but surely they could be of some help. Or perhaps they were helping, but in the background. He just wouldn't know about it.

If Martin had been on his way back to the hostel he would have taken the road that went over the bridge. Dag had already walked that route. But if Martin had been somewhat drunk he might simply have had an accident. What if he had tripped and fallen, perhaps into the river below. Or, if followed, could simply have been attacked and pushed over. The thought was one he didn't really want to contemplate.

Dag stood up determined to search the route again.

He walked back to the bridge. It was only a narrow roadway with no pavement and a low metal barrier on either side. The river was wide but not too deep but flowed quite strongly. The water was crystal; clear and he could see to the bottom. It flowed under another, larger bridge, to the fjord only about five hundred meters away. It would have been easy for anyone to trip and fall or, indeed, for a vehicle to have hit someone on the bridge and for a walker end up in the river. If they did, the body would quickly flow downstream to the fjord.

Dag turned right off the bridge and followed the road along the bank to the fjord surveying the river as he went in the hope that he might see something. He came to the end of the road, into a coach park and then to the spit of rock at the very end of the river. He saw nothing. If anything had floated this far it would have entered the fjord and that was deep, very deep indeed. It had to be deep, there was an extraordinary large cruise ship tied up alongside the opposite wharf which must have had draught meters deep.

He looked back upstream.

He knew well enough that whoever was behind the murder and the body's vanishing, and who was after Johan and his cousin, had no compunction about killing someone. He had to believe that it wasn't the case with Martin, but that he was being held somewhere. Where would he be held? It wasn't an overly populated place; there couldn't be many places to hold someone. Although, on the other hand, the hills and mountains around, as he knew, had scattered hunting and trekking huts any one of which may be difficult to find.

There were two people that might have an idea. The Cockerel's owner and the taxi driver. Theo had already told him that he knew of such places. And a taxi driver would know almost everything about the place.

He walked back along the bank to the main bridge and crossed over into the town and on to the station. The taxi driver, if he wasn't there, would turn up within a short time. His fares would not take him very far.

Dag waited in the nearby cafe topping up on caffeine. In twenty minutes the taxi parked up by the station. Dag finished his drink, went over, and slipped into the back.

The taxi driver gave out a deep sigh. "You again! Can't a man earn a living in peace?"

"Just need to pick your brains for a few minutes that's all. A bit of local knowledge. You probably know more about the area than anyone, all taxi drivers do."

"Very well. What do you want to know? The sooner we get it over with, the quicker I can get back to work."

Dag had an idea and asked him about the farms and their barns and outbuildings. Were there any that were empty, rarely used?

"Plenty of them. Most around here just keep the farms going as a hobby. No-one does it as a business these days; the tourists pay our wages and they like to see the farms looking in use. And the government grants give a steady little income."

"Any in particular that haven't been used for a long time? Maybe a farm that's not being used, derelict?"

"One or two. But further out on the Flåmsdalsvegen. It follows the river all the way up nearly to Myrdal."

Dag had the tourist map in his pocket."Can you show me on this?"

The taxi driver took it, looked and said, "This isn't much good, doesn't show any detail. But there's two place out on that road about there." He said pointing.

"Ok thanks, that will have to do for now. I'll match it to the map on my phone."

"You reckon those lads might be out there?"

"It's possible but my first job now is to find my partner." Dag answered as he got out of the taxi.

He had thought he might get the taxi driver too take him there that moment but resisted. He needed a car and a quick look at the tourist brochure showed there was a car rental firm on the road leading out of town. He would make his way there but first he needed to phone Rolf. He had to find out what was happening to his so-called support. Where was it? Why couldn't they give him some help? He felt that he'd need it. He had his weapon but otherwise he'd be on his own, and he didn't think it would be a good idea to go blundering to place not knowing what he'd be up against.

Rolf answered within a few rings.

Dag told him firmly that he needed help. His chances of finding Martin on his own were not good. His Detective Constable would be there the next day but she was young and inexperienced and he would be putting her and therefore him at greater risk. And if Rolf's assurances that there was E14 support close at hand now was the time he could use it. The fact that Martin was missing was taking the investigation away from finding Johan and Jørgen which was supposed to be their main objective.

Rolf assured him that he was aware of the difficulties he faced. And agreed that Martin's disappearance was complicating the issue. An agent was close at hand but he could not bring them out from undercover and have direct contact with Dag. The agent was fully aware of the events as they were unfolding and Dag must trust him that, if it came to it, they would intervene on his behalf. He would not be left in the lurch. And, he was of the firm belief that finding Martin would, in its turn, lead to the discovery of Johan and Jørgen.

The call ended.

'What now?' Thought Dag. 'The car rental firm. I've got to have transport.'

There was time to get to the hire firm and sort it out but it was already early afternoon and the sun would be setting by 17.20. After that he'd not be to investigate any farmsteads. It would have to wait until the next day. Yet another night that Martin would be missing. But at least Jenny would arrive.

He picked up a car and drove back to the hostel. He showered and changed. He looked though Martin's things in a vain hope that there'd be some clue; he may have returned without waking Dag. But, no, there was nothing. He was hungry and needed a drink There was one obvious place to go; The Cockerel.

The place was busy. The cruise ship was still in tied up and the more adventurous tourists were spending time on land. Dag was surprised that more of them weren't about, so many seemed to remain within the luxury and comfort of the ship taking in the view from the windows.

Sigurd and Sven were on the bar as before. He ordered a drink and a lamb stew then managed to find a seat at a table at the back of the room. Two other people were sat there; American tourists by the sound of them, but they didn't seem to mind his presence. As he was finishing his meal they excused themselves and left. As they passed through the main door another person walked in. It was Rita. She sauntered to bar, dressed in the red number, and ordered a drink. The boys could not help but both smile and try to talk to her at the same time hoping for her attention. But once she sipped her drink and had completed the pleasantries she looked around the room, checking out the patrons and, Dag presumed, the seating arrangements in case there was a free table. Her eyes swung around from the entrance, along the side wall and settling on the rear of the room where Dag sat; now on his own.

She gave him a strange look and turned and said something to Sigurd. Dag noticed that her smile had faded as she did so. One more sip of her drink and she turned towards him. With her eyes steadfastly holding his she walked purposely to his table.

Standing before him she asked. "May I?" Although her glass was already being placed down.

Before he could wave his hand to agree she had sat down.

"All on your own tonight?" She asked.

"Yes. I believe you met my partner last night?"

"Partner. A quaint term."

"Business partner. We work together."

"And what sort of work would that be?"

Dag pulled out is ID and showed her.

"Oh, you're police. He didn't act like a cop. And he's not here tonight?"

"No, unfortunately he's gone missing."

She gave him a strange look whilst sipping her large gin and tonic through a straw. "Missing? And you don't know where?"

"That's correct. And I believe you may have been one of the last people to see him; here last night."

"We sat here together, yes. Talked and had a drink. But I left on my own and he was still here."

"Yes, that's what the barmen have confirmed."

She gave a slight smile. "Asking questions about me, investigating me eh?"

Dag decided that his previous reluctance to interviewer her was now passed and changed tack. "You left the hotel this morning, checked out, but you've returned."

She smiled again. "My, you have been busy. Yes that's true. A girl can change her mind can't she?"

"You must have had a reason."

She took another sip of her drink. "I came here to meet someone. There was a change of plan but after I left the plan changed again on my way to Myrdal so I turned around and came back. We'll be meeting tomorrow."

"I see. Business?"

"She shrugged. "A mixture."

"A little pleasure as well then."

"Why not ... all work and no play."

"You didn't see my colleague after you left, then?"

"As I said, I left him here. I went back to the hotel; alone."

Dag drank back the remains of his drink. "Well, thanks for your help, but I must be going, I've a lot to do, I won't find Martin sat here."

"I hope you find him. And safely. Good night ..... ?" She looked at him questioningly.

"Dag, Dag Meldel; Detective Inspector Dag Meldel."

"Good night Detective Inspector Dag Meldel."

Dag walked away and out into a chill night. He wasn't sure what to make of Rita. But he knew what his stomach told him; and that was not to trust her.

*

The hours passed. Martin had dozed off from time to time. On and off he thought he heard a noise close by but despite straining his ears would hear nothing more. The throbbing in his head had subsided but he had a general dull ache and was thirsty again and hungry. The beam of sun that had caught his cheek had long since passed over him and he could fell that the temperature was falling. At least that gave him some relief.

There was a noise. This time it was real. He heard the door open again. He held himself as upright as he could.

The same procedure followed as before. The tape was removed and he was given water. He bent his head to the bottle and drank it.

"Why are you doing this?" he croaked. "Why keep me here?"

There was no reply.

""If you want to be done with me why keep me alive? You must have a reason."

Still there was silence. But a gloved hand took the bottle and substituted it with what was a sandwich; food.

"You feed me and water me. You must have a reason to keep me alive, to keep me here."

The hand pushed the sandwich towards his mouth. He stopped talking and ate. Then, when he'd finished, the hand gave the water back to him. He drank again.

"Thank you. You at least have some kindness in you."

At that the hand took the bottle away. He heard the sound of new tape being pulled from a roll and it was soon back over his mouth. He didn't even bother to complain or struggle. What was the point. If he acted reasonably maybe so might they.

He wished he had been partly released if only to be able to have a piss. He knew that the point would come he would have to simply wet himself. Footsteps moved back to the door and he heard the sound of it closing. Whoever it was simply left him there; in a matter of moments they were gone and there was silence. He was alone again.

*

Dag was being followed. The figure knew where he was staying. When Dag left to go to the Cockerel the figure moved openly to the hostel, casually entering the building where Dag had his room. There was no-one else about, all was quiet. And it didn't take long for Dag's room to be searched.

11.

Jenny had taken an early evening flight to Bergen and stayed overnight, then taken the first train to Voss and on to Myrdal and Flåm. She arrived at Flåm station at 10.35. Dag was there to meet her.

Drinking a coffee and having a late breakfast at the station cafe Dag briefed her on everything that had happened.

She looked into his eyes. "You don't really think the worst do you?"

"That he's dead? That he has either been in accident or killed? No I don't think so, I just don't get that feeling. I'm sure he's safe somewhere, or reasonably so. Even though we know that whoever's behind the murder of our mystery man would have no compunction in doing so. But if he's been kidnapped, held somewhere, why, for what reason?"

"The data; what Johan may still have on his computer."

"Yes. And what we might have on Martin's computer."

Jenny gave him a frown. "Martin's computer?"

"It's the one thing I've kept from you; from everyone else so far. We've got a copy on Martin's computer as well."

Jenny gave a look of surprise. "Where is it, have you got it here?"

"It's safe. But I've not got it, and neither has Martin, nor does he know where it now is. So even if he told someone it would no longer be where he thought it was. I don't even know exactly where it is myself."

"That must be what they're after. But what's the next move?"

"There's a number of empty barns and farm buildings around here so I've been told. That would seem to be the most likely sort of place to keep someone, and for our friends Johan and Jørgen to hide out. So, that's where we'll start. I've hired a car, there are places on the road out to Myrdal."

Dag's phone rang. He didn't recognised the number.

"D.I. Meldel." He said and listened. The answered. "Very well we'll right over."

"The local hotel." He told Jenny. "They've had a break in. It'll be some time for a local policeman to get here so they phoned me hoping I was still around. And I wouldn't be surprised if it's something to do with our case anyway. Let's go. You can leave your bag in the car for now, I've already arrange a room for you."

The night porter had gone on a round of the hotel as part of his security procedures at about 03.30. When he left reception he'd made sure he locked the door to the office and the key cupboard. When he returned after about twenty minutes he noticed that the door to the office was slightly ajar. The lock had been forced. He had looked in to the room and seen that paperwork had been knocked on to the floor and filing cupboard drawers had been opened. He very sensibly then kept out of it and phone Elise, the manageress. In the morning after talking to the nearest police station which was over forty kilometres away at Lærdal. They had limited staff and were only open three days a week in the mornings, and said no-one could be there until the afternoon, so she had thought of phoning Dag. She still had his number.

It was how Elise had described. Dag made sure he wore gloves and went into the office. He asked Elise to enter but not to touch anything.

"Can you take a look and see if there's anything missing. Where do you keep cash by the way."

"There in the safe." Elise pointed. "But it's still locked, doesn't look like it's been opened."

Dag went to check. It was firmly locked.

"They've just made a mess of everything. What was the point?" She asked.

"What about the cabinets? They've been opened. Is there anything missing?"

She went over and looked. "It doesn't look like it; we only keep files, paperwork and records in them, plus suppliers brochures. That's all. I can't understand what anyone would be after. Customer's records maybe. Perhaps they thought we had their bank details or something."

"Maybe." Said Dag, but he had a feeling he knew what was being looked for. "Is Ingrid in today? I'd just like another word with her about Jørgen?"

"She'll be in soon, I've called her and asked her to come in. I'll have to get her to clear this mess up."

"We'll get a coffee in your lounge wait we wait for her then, if that's ok."

"I'll get some for you. And thanks for coming."

Ingrid got there just ten minutes later. Dag saw her coming through the lounge windows and intercepted her before Elise could take her to do the cleaning up.

He wanted to know if the computer was safely hidden away and hoped that she hadn't simply put it in one of the office cabinets. He need not have worried. She assured him that she hadn't and that it was still safe. Dag had to hope she was right, but had no wish to know at this point where it was.

Time was moving on. It was getting near midday. They only had the afternoon to begin their search of likely farm buildings. It was time to take the road out of town. It would be an old fashioned house to house enquiry.

The first side road took them to a development of houses, not farms, so they turned back. The next took them to a large farmhouse and outbuildings. They knocked at the door and asked the woman that opened it if she knew of any empty farms, barns or outbuildings along the road. She told them that their best bet was to take a side road 1.5k along the road near Håreina railway stop. It was a winding mountainside track with hairpin bends where there were a number of empty buildings or one's just used as holiday homes.

The mountains towered on either side of the river valley as they drove to the turnoff. And then it was along the winding track. The track headed up steep slopes to higher ground. To the left and further ahead towered the steep walls of the mountains, the track winding its way through only slightly less precipitous land. The first of the houses they came to looked occupied. They stopped at the one on the first of the hairpin bends. There were two cars parked outside so they expected someone to be there.

The asked the man who came to the door if he'd noticed any unusual activity, people or strangers coming and going, especially at odd times of the day or night.

He had thought about it and at first said no but then hesitated and told them that he had twice thought he'd heard a vehicle late at night, later than anyone would normally be taking the road. He didn't remember if it was either going up or going down the track so could have been coming or going from further up the mountain. They thanked him.

Dag felt that they may be on the right track; literally.

They continued up the mountain.

It was time to stop and check each place they came to. There was nothing to the next hairpin bend and then on to the next. Still no more buildings. They came to a turn off and could see a farmhouse and group of buildings in the distance so turned off to investigate.

It was a working farm. The farmer's wife was there and they asked the same questions. She too said she had seen some car's lights late one night heading further up the road. She thought it was unusual at the time.

They turned back to the track and carried on upwards.

They could see a little higher up the slope of the mountain a more significant set of farm buildings set in a patchwork of green fields pressed against the side of the mountain 's face. The turn off to them was someway further up.

Still the occupants had not seen or heard anything unusual. But they did mention that there were some old buildings some distance ahead that were used in the summer although they thought they were now empty.

The next farm was not far but the winding track was slow going and it was taking time to get to each location. It would not be long before the sun began to set behind the mountain peaks. There was a short driveway to the farmhouse.

As they parked the car a man came from the farmhouse. There was a barn and two other outbuildings.

Dag asked him if he was the owner. The man said he was. He was thin and gaunt with deep set eyes. He kept his hands in his pockets whilst Dag talked, he held himself stiffly and seemed tense.

"Is it still a working farm?" asked Dag looking around.

"Does it look like it? No, not any more. I try to keep it in a reasonable condition but there's no money in working the land this high up even with subsidies. But I'm loathe to get rid of it's been in the family for generations."

Dag nodded. It was the same story for many of the high farms.

Again he asked if there had been any unusual activity; if he'd seen or heard anything out of the ordinary.

"Funny you should ask. There've been a couple of times, late in the day or at night, when I could have sworn I've heard a car heading up the track. There's only one more farm further up and between me and them some old barns. And I know Arnt and his wife wouldn't be about at that time of day."

Dag felt he was getting close. "Thanks for that. You've been a great help. We'll take a look at those old barns. And, Arnt you say, he lives at the last farmstead?"

"That's right."

"Thank you again. Come on Jenny; let's take a look at those buildings."

They got back in to the car and set off.

Jenny said. "He seemed a bit nervous to me."

"Hmm, you'll get used to that. People are either nervous or worried when we come to the door or can't stop talking trying to be helpful; or simply being nosy. But, yes, he was a bit tense. Mind you, I don't expect he has too many visitors up here, it's a pretty lonely place."

The man watched them go. He stared at them for a few seconds. He turned and went back into the farmhouse. A couple of minutes later he came out again. Not that he may have been recognised as the same person. He wore a long dark coat, gloves, and a balaclava.

*

"We can't stay here without food. I'm starving."

"Perhaps we can get some from that farmhouse down the road?"

"What, buy some, beg for some, and make them wonder who we are and what we're up to here?"

"Wait till there's no-one about. They don't lock their doors around here. We could easily sneak in and find something to eat."

Now it's breaking and entering or burglary if the door's open what's next on the list? Isn't it time we went back. We've been here long enough. It must be safe now. We could go to Bergen. A city's easier to hide out in. At least we'd be able to get food."

"They killed someone." said Johan. "They're after me, I know they are. And I don't think they're going to stop easily."

"Let them have it. Let's go back to Flåm. Get the computer from Ingrid and leave it somewhere, somewhere they can easily find it. If they're looking out for you, you could leave it in the open, make it obvious. They could take it and you'd be clear."

"Would I? I don't think so. I'd have to make sure they got it and I got away as well. And you for that matter. You know too much now. You'd have to get away as well."

Jørgen gave a deep sigh. "Shit, that's what you've git me in to; deep shit."

They were both silent. Johan couldn't think of a way to apologise. He realised he just hadn't thought it through when he'd come and asked Jørgen for help.

"All right." Johan said. "Let's go take a look at that farm. It's no good sitting here and starving."

He stood and made for the barn door. Jørgen lumped up. "I'll be glad just to get out of this place for a while anyway. Let's go."

The track was only a matter of twenty meters from the barn. Just as they reached it Johan stopped abruptly. He was looking along to the far hairpin bend. A car was driving up the slope towards it.

"Someone's coming." He said. "It's not the farmer's car."

"Let's get back."

""Not the barn; into the trees, we'll watch and wait till it pass, if it does. They ran back to the barn, passed it and then into the cover of trees on the downward slope. They waited listening to the sound of the car's engine as it came closer. As it got to their driveway the car turned and they could the sound of the wheels on the gravel surface. The engine stopped. They could now see it. The two car doors opened. A man and a woman got out.

Besides the barn there were two derelict buildings, once a small farmhouse and one a large shed. Their two visitors had a quick look at them and then turn to the barn.

"Our stuff's still in there." said Jørgen.

"We've hidden most of our stuff"

"Mostly, but it'll still be obvious someone's been there. And if they search they'll find our things, they're not hidden that well."

The man and woman went into the barn.

"We should get away, get going. If they find we've been there they'll start searching around. We can't stay here." Johan told him. "It looks like there's a bit of a track leading around this hill. It should take us to the road further down, near that farm perhaps."

Johan nodded. "Who do you think they are?"

"Whoever's after me that's who; who else? Come on let's go."

Dag and Jenny entered the barn. The door opened easily. They stood in its opening allowing their eyes to adjust to the darkness and then took a good look around before walking in.

"Looks like the place is being used." Dag said. "There's old straw about but it's flattened, someone's been here, and recently."

They both walked forward.

"You're right Sir, look there's some empty food wrappings."

Dag went over to them and turned them over.

"Take a look over there." He pointed to one side. "I'll look there." He said going towards the rear of the barn.

The rear was divided from the main area by an old animal stall. Behind it there was a heap of old straw heaped up against the dividing wall. Dag pulled it apart. Underneath and poorly hidden were two rucksacks.

"Here Jenny."

Jenny came over.

"Not difficult to find." He told her. "Two rucksacks mean two people. And we have two people missing."

He opened one rucksack, Jenny the other. Each had changes of clothes but nothing more.

"So, our two friends Johan and Jørgen have been hiding out here. Not who I wanted to find and not that we've found them of course."

"They must have seen us coming." Jenny ventured. "They seem to have left suddenly."

"Hmm, or they had left earlier for some other reason, which means they're likely to return. However, I think you may be right. They could have seen our car approaching form a long way off, it would have given them plenty of warning. They wouldn't have known it was us, the police, they'd have thought it might be whoever was after Johan. Which means they won't be far away. If you were them which way would you go?"

"Further on up?"

"Or back down the road. But we didn't see anyone. Let's take a look outside."

They walked around the old farm buildings and to the edge of the trees.

"Into the trees perhaps." Dag suggested. "They could even have watched us arrive.

Dag walked into a gap between the trees and started searching the area. Jenny followed.

"There Sir." She pointed. "Looks like a bit of a path. Just an animal track really. It's heading off down around the hill."

"Didn't know you were a country girl Jenny."

She smiled. "I wasn't brought up in town Sir, out in the countryside much like this."

"Then they're heading back down to the road. Let's go and see if we can intercept them."

They went back to the barn first. Dag took the two rucksacks and put them in the back of the car and they headed back down the track.

Johan and Jørgen could, for the most part of their walk down through the trees, keep an eye on the track from a distance. They were half way to the farm below them when Jørgen halted. He had heard the sound of the car engine again. They looked back at the track from the shelter of trees and could see the car heading back down.

"Shit." Jørgen hissed. "They're on the way back down. They must have guessed which way we were going."

"We could go back" Suggested Johan.

Jørgen shook his head. "If they don't find us they could back. It won't be safe there. And now we don't have any of our things. Nothing to wear, nothing to eat, we've got nothing but what we're wearing. This is hopeless Johan."

Johan gave a deep sigh and his shoulder slumped and he was silent.

Jørgen tried to sound upbeat. "We'll just have to hide out near that farm for a while until its all clear. If they're not there they won't hang around. When it's safe we'll ask the farmer for help. We'll tell him we were out walking and got lost. He'll give us a lift back to town. Then," he said decisively, "we go to the police."

Johan thought about it for a moment. "All right." He agreed. "We can't go on like this. Let's carry on down to that farm."

Martin heard the door open again. He had not expected it so soon. He had been asleep and had not heard the earlier arrival of a car.

He heard the footsteps come towards him and stop to his rear. Hands reached down to where he was tied to the post. His restraint to the post was being undone. Although his hands were still tied, and his feet firmly so.

The hands grabbed hold of him from behind and from under his arms he was lifted up. He could barely stand. The person was strong. He tried to hop along as he was dragged across the barn floor. He tried to speak but his mouth was still firmly taped and only muffled incomprehensible words came from him. He was place back on the floor. The person moved a pace or tow in front of him. He tried to get up into a sting position. He heard the sound of what he thought was a door and then the slamming of it. But it wasn't the slam of a door shutting; it was the slamming down of a trapdoor against the floor.

The person took hold of him again. He was dragged a few meters forward. He felt himself sitting on the edge of a hole and his feet inside it. He was picked up under each arm again, pushed forward and over the hole. He hung in empty space for a couple of seconds. Then the arms holding him let go.

He fell. It may not have been far but he felt it. The floor was hard and it hurt his right ankle and winded him as he landed to one side. The trapdoor slammed shut.

He lay for a time getting his breath back. He felt the coolest and damp of what must be a cellar. He didn't need his eyes to know he was in darkness.

Johan and Jørgen continued along and down the winding and faint animal track. They watched the car from between the trees as they made their way. It grew smaller as it took the track away from their hideout, turned sharply around the hairpin bend and then headed down and closer to them as it headed towards the same farmhouse as themselves. After a short distance it disappeared behind the crest of the hill which they were circling by which time they were less than a hundred meters away from it. Within a few minutes they were at the road.

They decided to take the road and get as close as they could to the farm and then get back into the trees for cover. They could then make their way, still under cover, and see what was going on.

Dag and Jenny reached the driveway to the farm and parked up at the farmhouse. They went to the door and knocked. The farmer opened it drying his hands on a towel.

"Back so soon?"

"Yes. I need to ask you about the empty buildings up the road. You might have noticed some activity. I wondered if you could think more carefully, think if there's anything more to tell us, something you might not have recalled before. Have there been any walkers up here, hikers? Anyone you might have seen."

The farmer slowly shook his head. "I'm sorry I can't think of anything." Then added. "Actually, no, come to think of it, there was someone, but that was days ago. No, not just one person though: think it was two. Probably walkers. Didn't take much notice."

"Hmm. Well thanks." Dag nodded. "Do you mind if we have a look around? Just means we can clear the place and won't have to come back."

The farmer shrugged. "Of course, if you want, I've got nothing to hide. Help yourself."

Dag hesitated.

"You can look on your own. I've got things to do. I needn't get in your way."

"Thank you we won't be long, just a quick look."

Dag and Jenny turned and headed for the outbuildings. They looked into two large sheds. There was nothing much in them but old pieces of farm machinery, rusting away and clearly not used for a long time.

They went to the barn and pulled open the door. It looked more used than the sheds. The floor was scattered with straw and there were several animal stalls. But other than that it looked unused. They search around but found nothing.

"Nothing here." Jenny said.

"No, it was just on the off-chance that Johan and Jørgen may have holed up here without the framer knowing."

"Or with him knowing?"

"He sounded genuine enough. I doubt it."

As Dag was passing through the barn door he looked back. The sun was getting low and would soon be setting and its light was passing through the door and highlighting the straw strewn floor. There was a glint of light. He walked to where it was and bent down. He brushed aside some straw. Jenny came up behind him. On the ground was a small bunch of keys. Dag picked them up. There was a leather key fob and three keys. He recognised them.

"Keys." said Jenny.

Dag nodded and stood. "Martin's keys."

There was a sound behind them. They turned in unison. The barn door still stood open with the light of the sun pouring through. A figure was outlined in the beam. It walked forward a couple of paces. Dag's and Jenny's eyes adjusted to the light. They could see more clearly. The figure was dressed in black. The face was hidden by a balaclava. Dag's eyes caught the movement of the right hand. In it was a weapon and it was pointed at them.

"Turn around." said a deep voice.

Jenny hesitated but Dag told her to do as they were told. He knew that it would be no good to do anything other than what the man said. In this sort of situation you had to remain calm and not antagonise the aggressor. The only way out of such a situation was to be composed and go along with whatever the person wanted. And what he wanted, and who he was, was what Dag needed to find out. This may be a state of affairs that would take some time to play out.

"Lie down. Face down. Hands behind your backs."

Dag glanced at Jenny and nodded. They did as they were told.

The figure moved towards them. They heard some movement and ropes were thrown down landing in front of Jenny.

"Tie his wrists, tightly, then his ankles. Do as you are told."

Again Jenny glanced at Dag and he nodded to her. She got up.

"Slowly." said the figure.

She took the rope and tied Dag's wrists and then his ankles.

"I will check them. Now you; lie back down, hands behind your back."

Before checking Dag Jenny's wrist and ankles were tied.

"What's this all about?" Dag asked. "Who are you? You're not the farmer are you, he's not build. You realise we're police officers. If you stop this now, whatever the problem is can be sorted out."

"No questions, no answers."

The man searched through Dag's pockets and took his keys and his phone then pulled him to the post. He took some more rope and tied Dag to it. Then he did the same to Jenny. He walked over to a corner, threw the phones into a pile of straw then picked up a roll of thick black tape and pulled a length from it. He came behind Dag and sealed his mouth, then did the same to Jenny.

He looked at them for a few seconds. He seemed satisfied and simply walked back to the barn door closing it behind him.

Johan and Jørgen were behind the cover of trees overlooking the farmyard. The car had been parked near the house. There was another car behind and to the side of the farmhouse and must have belonged to the farmer. All seemed quiet.

"They must be inside." Johan said.

The sun was getting low. And bathing the buildings and yard in a soft orange-yellow glow.

"So," asked Johan, "what do we do?"

Jørgen shrugged and shook his head. "Don't know. Just wait until they go I suppose. Then when it's clear see if we can get some shelter and some food."

There was a sound from the barn.

A figure had appeared in the doorway and was shutting it. The figure turned and they could see it easily in the evening sun. The man was dressed all in black.

"What the hell?" Jørgen exclaimed.

"He's wearing a balaclava. And, shit, he's got a gun."

They both cowered further behind their cover. The man walked to the visiting car. He opened the rear doors and looked in. From it he took a rucksack. He opened it and looked through the contents. Then he reached in, took the second one and did the same. Once he checked them he threw them back in. Then he got into the driver's seat. The car engine turned over and it was then driven away behind the derelict shed and out of sight of road.

When the sound of the engine had died there was the slamming of a car door and the man reappeared, walked to the farmhouse and went in closing the door behind him.

Johan and Jørgen had been holding their breaths and now breathed again.

"What the hell's going on? And who the hell was that?" Jørgen said.

"How should I know? I thought it was the other two that were after us."

"Do you think he's killed them?"

"I didn't hear any shots, did you?"

Jørgen shook his head.

"He must have them in that barn." Suggested Johan.

"Yes, but who are they? Are they after you? And who's he?"

"There may be one way to find out."

Jørgen looked at him wide-eyed. "Are you mad? You're thinking of going down there?"

"When it's dark. Why not. We can't just leave it like this."

Jørgen shook his head again but said nothing.

12.

Rita had watched from her bedroom window as Dag and Jenny had pulled up to the hotel. She watched them enter and waited, sipping a cup of coffee. No more than twenty five minutes later she saw them go to their car and leave. She watched them turn left and drive along the main road out of town before they were hidden by the hill and trees behind the hotel. She made call on her mobile phone then got a coat and shoulder bag and made her way to reception.

"Was that the policeman I saw here again, I saw him from my window?" she asked Ingrid.

"Oh, yes, we had a break-in last night. Nothing to worry about though, it was the office here and they didn't take anything. Probably just tried to get into the safe but couldn't."

"Oh, that's not good. I hope the rooms are secure."

"Oh I'm sure they are. We've never had anything like it before. It's just a one-off, I'm sure of it. Maybe one of the workers from the cruise ship."

"Well, let's hope so." Rita paused. "But the police were here before that. Was that something else?"

"Oh, yes." Said Ingrid cautiously. "Someone's gone missing, he used to work here."

"And they're out searching for him?"

"Yes."

Rita gave a concerned look. "Oh dear, was he a friend of yours?"

Ingrid nodded.

"I'm sorry, I'm being nosy aren't I. You look upset, were you close, a boyfriend perhaps?"

"Not really, but I liked him."

"And you have no idea what's happened to him?" Ingrid shook her head again.

Rita smiled. "Well if need a bit of support just pop up to my room. It's always good to talk, not to keep things bottled up. We all need a shoulder to cry on once in a while. I know what it feels like. I can't tell you the times I've been let down by a man." She reached over and patted Ingrid on the hand. "Now, don't hesitate, if you need someone to chat to just pop up."

She smiled and handed over her keys.

Ingrid relaxed and smiled back. Thank you, yes, I'll remember that."

The call she made had been to hire a car and as she left the entrance the company was delivering it.

Dag and Jenny could have been heading back to their hostel, but Rita doubted it. She was sure they would be on the road leading out of town. And she would take the same road. She didn't have to hurry. She was able to track it. The night before she had had attached a tracking device to it.

She took the tracking monitor out of her bag and plugged it in to the car's charger; she didn't want it to lose power. The device lit up. The map filled the screen and a small pinpoint of light flashed to show the position of Dag's car. It was on the main road heading south. She started the engine and set off.

Dag was only a couple of kilometres ahead and within a few minutes his car had slowed and stopped. Rita slowed down. She didn't want to get too close as yet.

She pulled up to the side of the road and watched the map. Dag's car turned off the main road. It headed up what, on the map, hardly looked like a road at all but just a track. She pulled onto the road and carried on to the same point where she too turned off.

She could see the track winding up and along the hillside through the tree lined slopes until it turned away at a hairpin bend. And she could see Dag's car heading up it. Once again she halted and watched. Dag had pulled up at what, from her distance, looked like a set of farm buildings.

A few minutes later the set off again but went out of view behind the trees and hill.

She considered what to do. Obviously Dag had reason to be making enquires here. He must have got some information, either about Martin or perhaps the two missing young men. Either way it was information that she also needed. But how close should she get?

She took a better look at the map. The track went up into the mountains then petered out. Along the way it looked like there were a few small farms and maybe one or two small old buildings, probably abandoned. She didn't want to get too close and give herself away. Dag and Jenny could only go so far up the track and no further. If they found something it would be good news, not for them necessarily, but for her. Whatever happened, whether they found something or someone, or nothing at all, they would have to come back down the same track. There was no need for her to chase up there after them. She could let them do the work for her.

A little further up the road on a turn to the left the railway line from Myrdal to Flam passed over it. There was halt for the trains and a small building acted as waiting room for the few that stopped there. She decided to park near it and look as if she was waiting for a passenger. She could then spot Dag returning back down the track from its cover.

To begin with she sat in the car and watched the tracker. Dag's car carried on up the track stopping at some of the farms. He was getting close to the final farm and as far as the track went them stopped at what looked like some deserted buildings. He was there for a while. It piqued Rita's interest. Then the car set off back down the track. Had he found something or someone? The car got as far as the farm where it had stopped before and stopped again.

'Asking more questions there.' Rita thought.

The minutes ticked away, the car remained stationary.

Rita watched and waited as the time passed by. She looked at her watch. It was getting late. The sun was reaching down to the mountain peaks. It set early here with the mountains cutting it off earlier than on flat low ground. Still the car did not move.

'What are they up to?' she thought. "They must have found something; which means they must come back down soon. That is, if nothing had gone wrong.'

Suddenly the light moved. The car was in motion. But not for long. It stopped again; it had only gone a matter of meters.

She sat back and thought. 'They're not coming back down. What can it mean? There are only two possibilities. They are staying there for a reason of their own, or they are staying there against their will. Which is it?'

There was only one way to find out. And she need to get up the track and near that farm before the light faded. She didn't want to be using her headlights and completely giving herself away. She started the engine and set off.

It took her fifteen minutes to get close to the farm. She stopped on a straight stretch of track where there was some clearance of trees on the upward slope. It was about only about three hundred meters from the farm entrance but a dip in the road and the cover of the trees obscured the view of the farm and it of her.

She had taken the precaution of wearing good sturdy shoes. She checked the map on her tracker, and set off thought the trees on the downward slope of the hill towards the farm.

She found a position with a good view of the farmhouse. Dusk was coming. She took form her bag a large pair of binoculars. They had night vision ability although she didn't need that for the time being but it would soon be useful.

All appeared quiet. She moved back towards her left keeping under cover. Then she spotted the car parked to the side of an outbuilding. She recognised it; it was Dag's hire car. Dag and his new accomplice were there. But where; and why would they still be there after so much time? She focussed on the farmhouse. There was no activity that she could detect. Then she scanned the area around.

She spotted a slight movement in the trees opposite to her position, close to the road and overlooking the farmyard. She focussed on it. There it was again. It could be an animal, a deer perhaps. But then she thought she could make out a figure, in fact it could be two. If it was two she guessed who it could be; Johan and Jørgen.

She caught their movements as they disappeared to the right and in the trees behind the farmhouse. She waited. It was likely that they were circling around to where the car was parked by the shed. She kept her eyes peeled. Sure enough she spotted them again as they emerged from behind the farmhouse. She made a decision. She couldn't let them get to the car. They may escape; that may be their plan.

She quickly made her way around the edge of the tree cover to get to them. Getting near to them she came around and behind them. They had not yet moved. She reached into her bag again and this time pulled out a pistol. Quietly she crept forward. She was practised at such craftwork. When only matter of two meters from them her foot stepped upon a brittle twig and it snapped. Johan and Jørgen spun around. They faced her pistol.

"Keep calm, don't move and keep quiet." She told them.

Slowly she allowed the pistol to come down.

"Sorry to surprise you like that. You're in no danger and I don't intent to harm you. I'm on your side. I'm from E14, military intelligence. Let me show you." She added as she reached into the bag and pulled out an identity card.

She walked two paces forward and held it up for them to see.

"I think it's time we helped you get out of this mess you've got into. But first, what's going on here?"

Johan and Jørgen stared at the woman. Both their hearts had almost stopped beating when she'd surprised them. They were both too shocked to move. But when she showed them her ID they relaxed.

"Jesus Christ you scared me!" Jørgen exclaimed.

"Keep your voice down." Rita hissed. "Now, answer my question. What's going on here?"

Jørgen looked at Johan. Johan looked back at Rita. He told her that two people had been taken to the barn by a man dressed all in black. His face was covered with a balaclava and he was armed.

Rita nodded. "I know who they are, and I can guess who the man is. We need to get you away from here. And I'm going to need support to get them out of there. I'm not going to do that on my own. I've got a car parked further down the road. I can get you away to safety. Then I can sort things out here. First things first. We'll circle back around to the road. Now, no talking, no arguments, just do what I say. OK?"

The two of them nodded. They were only too pleased that at last they were in safe hands and had no intention of arguing with her.

"Don't worry we'll follow you. I've had enough of all this." Said Jørgen.

"Me too, I just want it all over now. But who're the two he took inside? We were going to help them."

"Don't worry about them for now. As I said I'll get back-up and whatever's happening here will be sorted out. Now let's go."

It didn't take long to get back to the end of the drive and the track.

For a brief moment they had to cross it in the open before they were again hidden by the trees.

The man was keeping an eye out from a bedroom window at the side of the farmhouse. The light was fading but he had good eyesight and was use to the conditions. He was watching the track beyond the driveway. Suddenly there was movement. Figures had come from the cover of the trees and dashed across a small gap of open ground at the drive entrance. Two, no three of them. They disappeared down the track.

He grabbed his balaclava and pulled it over his head and at the same time was running from the room and leaping down the stairs several steps at a time. In the main room he passed the farmer tied to a chair with mouth taped. He ran across the yard to the barn and roughly pulled open the door.

He ignored Dag and Jenny and went to the back of barn.

Dag and jenny heard the barn door flung open. They heard the man run passed them and then stop. Dag made out the sound of straw being moved and then the loud bank of what sounded like a door being opened; a trap door perhaps. He had not thought of looking for that.

The man jumped down into the cellar.

Martin came wide awake. He felt someone's arms behind him a-under his arms. He was being pulled up.

"Up the steps." The voice said. And he was being dragged up them. He tried to get his feet onto the rungs and help himself.

He was out of the cellar and being dragged along the floor trying at the same time to move his tied feet in a hopping motion. Then he was dumped back down on the ground.

I was only then he saw two more bodies. Two more people tied and gagged. He felt both relief and despair. It was Dag and Jenny. They too had been captured by this person; this person being a man, and a strong one at that.

The man said nothing but, to his surprise, reached down and untied his hands. He looked at them all for a brief second and then turned and ran off and out of the barn.

Martin rubbed his sore and bruised wrists.

Dag wriggled about and was trying to speak but only a muffled mumbling came out.

Martin pulled the tape from his mouth in one quick movement. It pulled against his lengthening stubble and stung him. He took in a deep gulp of air.

Form outside the barn they heard the sound of a car engine and then the sound of it driving off over the gravel drive and to the track.

With a dry throat Martin croaked. "All right, all right, give me a chance."

He set to untying the rope that held his legs. When it fell away he gave his ankles a firm rubbing and stretched his legs.

"All right, now you two." He said, crawling over to them.

First he removed the tapes.

"So he got you two as well did he?" He said as he began removing their restraints.

"I didn't even realise you were here. We were looking for Johan and Jørgen. We're sure they must have been holed up in an empty building further on up. We must have just missed them, their rucksacks were still there."

Marin had freed Dag's hands and he was untying the rope around his legs whilst Martin began on Jenny.

"Are you Ok Jenny?" Martin asked.

She nodded. "I'll be fine, just a bit shaken."

"Oh, I'll be fine as well." Dag muttered.

"Of course you will, boss."

Dag frowned and wrinkled his nose. "What's that smell?" Then gave Martin a god look up and down.

"If you'd been held here unable to go to the toilet, you'd end up in this state as well. There was nothing I could do about it." His voice almost gave out. "And I've got to get a drink." He added.

Dag and Jenny stood up. Martin had some difficulty and Dag grabbed him to help him on his feet.

"What I don't understand is why he's suddenly let us go and run off." Dag mused.

"Perhaps help is on the way?" Suggested Jenny.

"Yes, maybe, let's hope so. Now let's go and take a look outside."

As they left the barn the final rays of the sun were descending behind the mountain ridge. Dag and Jenny walked easily but Martin was just hobbling along. The first thing they realised was that their car was not parked where they had left it. But glancing to his right Dag could just see the rear bumper of a car jutting out from behind one of the sheds. He jogged over.

"Our car, it's here."

"First a drink." Martin almost pleased.

Dag nodded. "The farmhouse. You go with Jenny. I'll take a look around."

He checked out the car. The rucksacks were still in the back and everything seemed as it was. There must have been another car they hadn't noticed when they arrived. He reached into his pockets for the keys. They weren't there. The man must have been a bit of a pickpocket for Dag not to have noticed he'd taken them. But they'd have to get the car started somehow.

He heard Martin and Jenny emerging from the farmhouse and went back around the shed.

They had the farmer with them, the man who# come to the door and spoken to them.

"He'd been tied up to a chair and taped." Explained Martin. "Held hostage."

"Your safe now Sir." Dag assured him. "Did he give you any idea why he did it, what he was up to?"

The man shook his head. "When he first turned up he showed me ID, said he worked for the Government, something secret. I was to help him and not ask any questions. He was after some bad people."

"And then?"

"I got suspicious. Started asking questions. I didn't want him here. I wanted him to leave. That's when he pulled out the gun and tied me up. When you came he said he'd kill me if I didn't play along. I didn't have any choice."

"Of course not, you did the right thing. And don't think of blaming yourself for anything. But what we have to do is get away from here and back to Flåm. Perhaps you should come with us?"

He shook his head emphatically. "No thanks. I'll be fine. I just want to be alone here if it's all the same."

"Very well, if that's what you'd prefer, but if you need any help or counselling, someone to talk to, then I'll give you a number to ring. We heard a car, was that his?"

"It must have been mine, he took my keys. He's stolen my car!"

"We'll do what we can to get it back for you. He's taken our keys as well and we need to get our car started." Dag added looking around at them all. "Any ideas?"

"Let me look." Sid the farmer. "I know my way around cars. Mine's always needing work to keep it going."

"It's round the side of the shed." Dag told him.

The farmer lifted the bonnet. "I just need couple of tools" he said and went to the shed.

He was out and under the bonnet again and, suddenly the car's engine burst into life and he slammed the bonnet down.

"There you go."

"I don't know how to thank you." Dag said shaking by the hand.

"Find that bastard and sort him out."

Dag smiled. "I promise you I will, and we'll be back to let you know. Here," Dag wrote down his own number on a small piece of paper, "this is my number, any problems just give me call."

"Are you all right to drive?" Dag asked Martin.

"Oh, I can drive all right." Martin said firmly.

Dag and Martin jumped into the front and Jenny into the back.

The wheels spun on the gravel as Martin backed up the car and then again as he accelerated forward. Moments later they were on the track and Martin was practicing his rally driving. Dag was used to it, Jenny pushed herself into the seat and half closed her eyes.

"He said he was E14 by the sound of it." Martin pointed out.

"Yes, sound like our man who stole the memory stick from the police station. Jan, Vaižgantas , Patrik, whatever his real name might be. And our killer as well, I'm sure."

"I still don't understand why he didn't just leave us there, why he freed me? Why? It doesn't make sense. If he's a professional killer he could have just got rid of us there and then."

"I don't know." Replied Dag. "A pang of conscience? No, I doubt it. And we won't find out unless we find him. "

Rita kept a close eye on the track behind her. She couldn't see anyone following. The light had almost faded and if anyone followed her now she should soon see the lights of any vehicle.

"I'll take you to the hotel." She said. "It'll be safe there. Is there anyone you know who can help you? That young girl in reception maybe?"

"Ingrid?" Jørgen asked. "Yes she should have made sure my room's still there for me."

"You know who she is?" asked Johan.

"I've been staying there, at the hotel. As a tourist, a good enough cover story. I was talking to her this morning. She seemed worried, upset. Concerned about you I think, Jørgen. She really seems to like you."

Jørgen blushed slightly. "Yes, I think she does."

"Let's back there and get you two together then." Rita smiled looking at him in the rear view mirror. As she did so she saw tow lights break through the gloom further up the mountainside. She was coming to the turn off onto the main road. There was no traffic and she turned sharply onto it. Her foot pressed further onto the accelerator and they sped into town. Within five minutes they were parking outside the Hotel.

The farmer's old car was not fast, neither was it particularly roadworthy. The man had to take care as he went down the mountain track. And he went for as long as he could without lights; he didn't want to attract attention. But the driving became too difficult and without them he was slowing down so he had no choice but to turn them on.

His quarry had a head start and would probably be gaining on him but there were only two ways they could take once they got to the main road and the only one they were likely to take was to Flåm.

Rita almost screeched to a halt in front of the hotel.

"You two stay here for a moment. I'll just make sure everything's clear, you never know."

She didn't give them time to think or reply before she was out of the car and heading for the entrance. Elise was on reception.

"Good evening." Rita smiled.

"Oh, Ms Hustad, you're back again?"

"I'm not staying. I just needed a word with your receptionist, Ingrid. I have something to tell her about Jørgen. Is she about?"

"Jørgen? You've heard something?"

"Yes I bumped in to the police officers, they told me the young men were safe and sound. I said I was coming this way so I'd let Ingrid know. She seemed very fond of him when I talked to her earlier. Is she about?"

"Well that's a relief. She's only this minute finished. She went out the back." Elise said indicating the door to the kitchens.

"Would you mind? I won't be a nuisance, but if I could just pop through. It's just that I promised to tell her personally, and I wouldn't want to be remiss." She smiled.

"Elise relaxed. "Oh well, it's such good news, and I can't leave the desk. Yes, go on, she should be through there, probably talking to the head chef."

"Thank you, you're so kind." Rita beamed broadly. And she headed to the door.

There was just one person in the kitchens. He must have been the head chef. He looked surprised when she came in and frowned.

"It's Ok, Elise gave me permission." She said and smiled sweetly. "I was looking for Ingrid. She came this way?"

"She's just out the back." He told her pointing to a door. "Having a cigarette."

"Thank you. You're a dear." She said as she gently touched his arm.

The chef reddened. "No problem." He muttered, and watched her as she went to the door and through it.

Ingrid was outside just finishing her cigarette.

"Ingrid! I've found you. Good news!" Rita said with her broad smile. "Jørgen and Johan, they've been found safe and well. The police asked me to came here and tell you, they were tied up with something else. One of their men is missing I believe. They're not far away; I'll go and get them. They just wanted to make sure you were here"

Ingrid's face lit up. "Jørgen's been found? And he's OK? Oh, that's great, where is he?"

I'll go and get him right now! Oh, and Johan said something about – 'can you get the laptop' – he said he needed it, it was very important. He wanted it as soon as he could meet you. Do you know what he means?"

"Yes, yes, I do. I've got his laptop, its inside."

"Well, pop off and get the thing I'll go and pick up Jørgen and Johan. I won't be long. We'll meet back here."

Ingrid dashed back through the door and into the hotel. Rita's smiled vanished and she walked swiftly around the side of the building to the parked car. She breathed a sigh of relief to see Jørgen and Johan were still waiting inside. She opened the door and smiled warmly.

"All clear. And I've just spoken to Ingrid. She's relieved you're both safe, especially you Jørgen. I said we'd meet her around the back. We didn't want to disturb Elise in reception."

The two of them got out of the car.

"I'll come with you." Rita said. "I like to see a happy ending. No tears mind you, let's only have smiles."

No sooner had they got to the rear door than it opened and Ingrid appeared.

"Jørgen, Johan! You're here! And you're OK?" she asked.

"Of course we are." Jørgen told her. "You needn't have worried, we were safe enough."

Johan was staring and frowning at Ingrid. "That's my laptop."

"Yes, Rita said you wanted it."

Johan looked at Rita.

"Yes, I thought you'd want it." She said at the same time holding out her hands to take it from Ingrid.

Without thinking Ingrid put it into Rita's hands. Johan was about to hold out his hands to take it from her but she took a step backward.

"Thank you." Rita said smiling.

"Give that to me. It's mine!" Johan called out, and took a step towards her.

Rita took another step back. "I think not."

"Stand still all of you!" Came a voice from the side of the building.

Johan, Jørgen and Ingrid automatically looked around. The voice had come from behind them. Rita could see who it was.

A man stood at the corner of the building. And he had a gun in his hand.

"Do not move, any of you. And not word, not a sound. I can assure you I've killed before and would not hesitate to do so again." He paused and smiled. "Well done Rita my dear."

Johan, Jørgen and Ingrid turned back to face Rita. She was smiling at the man. "It all went perfectly Jan. Or is it another name today."

"Jan will do nicely." The three turned to him again. "Now, you three, I don't want to hurt you, so I'll give you a chance to get out of this with your lives. You're going to take a walk. Over there." He pointed with the gun in his hand to the hillside and trees to the rear of the hotel. "Start walking, keep walking, go into the trees and don't look back. I'll be watching and waiting. Stay there for at least five minutes, don't look back. If you do I'll use this. Now, get moving." He waved his gun. "I said get moving, and quickly, I don't intent wasting time. Move!"

Jørgen grabbed Ingrid's arm. "Come on, do as he says. Johan, it's no good, let's go."

Red walked towards the wooded slope.

As they got to the trees the man shouted. "That's it, keep going, and don't look back."

"Come on." He said to Rita. "Move."

They ran around the side of the hotel, Rita still grasping the laptop, and in moments were in the car. The engine sprang to life and with a squeal of the tyres they were off turning left heading to the main road.

"I thought she was nice." Ingrid said with tears in her eyes.

They waited for five minutes in the shelter of the trees not saying anything, not knowing what to say.

"Come on." Johan said, after the time had elapsed, "Let's go."

"He said to wait. He could kill us." Ingrid told him with fear in her eyes.

"They're not going to hang around are they?" Johan answered. "As soon as we were in the trees they'd be off. Come on."

Johan ran back out of the trees. Jørgen and Ingrid followed. There was no sign o the man and Rita but they heard the sound of a car racing away from the hotel.

"Come on." Johan urged them. "We need a car. Is there one we can use Ingrid?"

"A car?"

"Yes, a car."

"Elise has got one."

"You're not thinking of going after them!" Jørgen exclaimed.

"They've got the laptop. If I can't get it back I've at least go to know where they're going. I've got to follow them."

"You're mad."

But Johan was already in the back door hand heading for reception.

Elise was still behind the counter. Jørgen and Ingrid caught up with him.

"Ingrid says you've got a car. We need it!"

Elise stared at him almost in shock. "I beg your pardon."

"We must have a car. We've just had something stolen, something very important. We're helping the police." He added. "They'll be here soon but there's no time to lose. Can we borrow you car?"

"It's true." Ingrid pleaded. "They need it. Please let them borrow it. Please Elise, please, its' urgent and important. The police will confirm it. Please let them borrow your car." Ingrid pleaded again.

Elise was shaking her head. All right, I believe you. I've just had another man in asking about Rita. He showed me ID, the security services or something. She'd just left in her car. I soon as I told him he was out of the door and off."

Elise sigh and her hand went to her bag at her side. She gingerly pulled out a set of keys. "If anything happens to it ...."

She didn't have time to finish before Johan had grabbed them and was off.

"It's the blue Toyota RAV." Rita added.

"Ingrid, stay here." Johan was shouting. "Jørgen, are you coming?"

Jørgen set off at a run following him out into the car park looking out for the blue car.

Rita and Jan sped off. As they disappeared another car sped into the car park. It was the farmer's car. The man dashed out and in to the hotel. Only thirty seconds later he was back in the car and setting off again, following the same road as Rita and Jan.

The car slid to one side as Martin rounded the last of the hairpin bends. The car almost came to a stop. Martin tugged at the steering wheel and corrected their trajectory. Dag had his arms out in front of him holding the dashboard and Jenny grasped her seatbelt as tightly as she could.

"It won't be much good if we don't get where we're going." Dag complained.

"Sorry boss."

They sped forward again, screeched to a halt at the main road and had to wait for a small succession of cars and two lorries going in either direction before they could pull out. It seemed to take an age. But then they were on their way to Flåm. The sun had now set and darkness was falling.

They came towards the hotel. As they did so Dag was sure he'd seen a car's lights disappear around the bend ahead. But before he could think any more about it Martin was pulling in to the car park. All three jumped out and in to reception. Elise was still at the desk.

"You as well!" she declared. "What on earth's going on?"

She paused and looked at the state of Martin and screwed up her face in an expression of some disgust.

"Don't ask." Martin told her.

"Us as well?" Asked Dag.

"Everyone's rushing in and out today."

"Who. Quickly now. Tell us."

"Well, first that woman Ms Hustad. Then another man said he was security or something. He showed me ID. Then Jørgen and Johan turned up. They've taken my car."

At that point Ingrid appeared from the office.

"Ingrid?" Dag queried.

"Rita she and another man. He had a gun. He threatened to kill us. We had to go into the woods until they went."

"Let's go." Dag told Martin and Jenny.

They turned.

"Oh," Ingrid called as they left, "they took Johan's laptop."

Dag paused at the door. "They took the laptop."

"Yes, I'm sorry I got it for her. I thought she was giving it back to Johan."

"Don't worry we'll get it back for them."

They sprinted to the car and were back on the road.

"Which way?" Martin asked.

"That way." Dag pointed to the left. "A car sped off that way just as we arrived. Our man from the farm I expect."

"But he said he was with security and showed ID."

"Yes, our man who stole the memory stick, I'm sure of it now."

"But Rita and this other man with her. He was armed and they've got the laptop."

"E14? Let's hope so. I wouldn't like to think anyone else is involved in all this"

They were coming towards the docks and the lights of the cruise ship that had been moored there lit up the entire scene.

Dag suddenly felt his stomach tighten. It knotted again as it did so often when some strange instinct kicked in. They were about to pass the dock car park and on to the tunnel that bored its way through five kilometres of solid rock.

"Stop!" Dag shouted.

Martin hesitated and looked at him.

"Stop!" Dag repeated. "Let me out."

Marin slammed on the brakes and veered to the side of the road coming to a halt.

"What? What is it?" Martin asked.

Already Dag was opening the door and getting out.

"You carry on. Find Rita, the killer, or at least find the boys and make sure they're safe. Get going!"

"But ..." Martin began.

"Go!" shouted Dag as he slammed the door shut.

Martin shook his head. He would do as he was ordered. But he couldn't understand what Dag was up to. His foot hit the accelerator and the car shot forward towards the tunnel opening. He could only imagine that Dag had one of his famous intuitions.

Five kilometres beyond the exit of the tunnel the farmer's car came to a stop. The man sat in it making a phone call. This car had no chance catching up with Rita. He would need support. He'd not been able to use his phone for much of the time in the mountains, the signal had been so poor, and so had been out of touch. He needed to get further instructions. He needed Rita and whoever she was with to be stopped. He couldn't do it on his own.

As he finished his call a blue car sped past him. He watched the rear lights as it went ahead. The he noticed that it was slowing. The car was pulling up ahead of him just before turning a corner. If it had gone further it would have been out of his sight.

Someone had followed him. But who? It must be the prisoners who'd have released themselves. But it wasn't the same colour as their car. And he still absolutely sure who they were. Although he was now realising that they might not be who he at first feared.

The car was turning around.

He would wait. He'd made his phone call and help was on the way and it wouldn't take long for them to be there.

It drove back towards him but then stopped some one hundred meters away.

"We can't get out of the car. We can't do anything. If it's him from the farm he's armed." Jørgen warned Johan.

"I know. I'm not sure what to do. Perhaps we should have just carried on, after Rita."

"But like you said, she's got a head start we might never catch up with her."

"And," added Johan in a perplexed tone, "if she's the enemy, then who's he?"

"I don't know. It's all too confusing. Let's just go back to the hotel."

Martin sped through the tunnel and out into the open. He was easily breaking the speed limit. In just two and a half minutes he reached the point where the two cars were parked on either side of the road.

Immediately he knew that these were cars he was following. His foot hit the brakes. They screeched, rubber burned and the car slithered to a stop some two hundred and fifty meters passed the farmers car, a hundred and fifty passed Johan and Jørgen. He twisted the steering wheel, hit the accelerator and drove back.

Johan and Jørgen had watched him. They saw him coming back along the road towards them. At the last moment he served to their side of the road, For a moment they though he was going to crash into them. But he braked and came to a stop with centimetres from their front bumper. A man got out and came to them. He knocked on the door's window.

Johan looked out at him. The man was a mess. The man knocked again and indicated that he wanted him to open the window. He held an ID up for Johan to see. It was the police. Johan opened the window. The man smelt.

The farmer's car had stayed where it was, unmoving.

"Yes?" asked Johan.

"Let me guess, which one are you Johan Christiansen or Jørgen Arnesen?"

Dag ran across the car park. The cruise ship was about to leave. Any moment the gangplank would be rolled back onto the ship and it would be off, slipping away from its moorings. And Dag had a strange feeling that somebody else would be slipping away with it. He didn't know why he thought it only that the knot in his stomach and his intuition was telling him so. What better ruse to play. The most obvious thing that Rita could do was to escape by road, but to Dag the more obvious and clever bit of subterfuge was another means of escape, the cruise ship, who would think she and her companion were in that.

He raced across the car park. The gangplank was lifting. It had gone a half meter. He jumped. Almost slipped on its slipper steel surface but managed to keep on his feet. And he scrambled up onto the deck.

A furious ships officer was watching him.

"Who the hell do you think you are? What do you think you're doing? You could have killed yourself."

Dag reached into his pocket and pulled out his ID.

"Police."

The officer took a good look at it. "Oh I see." He said more quietly. "What's it about? You were in a hell of a hurry."

"I think there's someone on the ship I need to question, Two people in fact, a man and a woman. The man could be dangerous."

"Dangerous?" the officer sad with a frown. "How do you mean?"

"Nothing for you to worry about for now. Tell me, did an man and a woman come aboard just before I did, at the last minute. They'd be the last people to come back aboard."

"There was a couple came aboard just five minutes or so before you. I told them they were cutting it fine. Not as fine as you mind."

"Do you know where they went?"

The officer shrugged. "They had a boarding pass; I didn't look closely enough to see which cabin they were in."

"Then I'll have to look around. Tell the Captain I'm aboard and to get a message to this number." He looked at his phone for Rolf's number. "You've got a pen and paper?"

"Yes."

Dag gave him the number. "Just ask him to get a message to that person. Tell them I'm aboard and that I am close." Dag didn't want to be distracted by making the call himself.

"That you are close?"

"That I'm close."

"Very well Sir. I'll go now."

Already Dag could hear and feel the throb of the engines. Most of the passengers, he imagined, would be on the decks watching the lights of Flåm receding into the darkness before the prepared for dinner.

Martin looked at the farmer's car. In it would be the man who'd held him hostage.

"Stay here and don't move." He told them.

Marin walked purposely towards the car. It took him a minute or so to walk the distance. He stopped a few meters from it. The headlights had remained on until then and he was dazzled by them and could make nothing out. As he halted the headlights turned off leaving just the side lights on. The door opened and did so the indoor light came on and he could see the man who'd held him. He swung himself out of the seat and stood behind the open door. Martin thought he could see the gun in his hand.

Martin carefully, first holding his arms out to show he was unarmed, put his right hand into an inside pocket and pulled out his ID. The man had not for it or found it before. He walked one step forward and held it is outstretched hand for the man to see. It should have been clear what is was in the car's lights.

"Police." The man said.

"Detective Sergeant Sorensen." Martin told him.

"I mistook you for someone else. I wondered if I'd been wrong about you." The man replied. "The other two?"

"My colleagues."

"Ah, I see. I hadn't been sure and couldn't take any chances. Apolgies."

The man's hand came from behind the car door. He wasn't holding his weapon. He too held up an ID. Martin took a final step towards him to take a close look; E14.

"You may call me Rune." He said.

"Who the hell did you think I was?"

"The man we're after of course. Unfortunately my communications went down. I'd not heard anything from central for more than twenty four hours before you arrived. You were on your own. You could easily have been the one, although

I was also here to keep an eye on you and your colleagues if you got into difficulties."

"Great. What now?"

"I've made contact. Help is on the way. My tanks just about dry I don't think I'd get much further."

"And Rita and her friend will be well ahead of us now."

"They'll find them. They're on the road and there's a chopper in the air."

As he said it they could both hear the sound of an aircraft in the distance. Martin turned and waved to Johan and Jørgen calling them to him. Their car lights brightened and they drove slowly forward stopping just a few meters away.

The sound of the aircraft's engine grew. It was clear to Martin that it was a helicopter. Suddenly its lights burst over the ridge of the mountain and it came towards them. It slowed and hovered for a moment.

Rune's phone rang and he answered it. He listened and simply said, "Very well, Sir."

Then the helicopter turned away and sped off over the mountain that encased the tunnel and on to Flåm.

"We've got to go. Your car." Rune said. "Back to Flåm. Quickly."

Martin didn't hesitate. He shouted to the two others to follow them.

'Dag.' He thought. 'Dag was still in Flåm. Dag was where the action was happening.' He should have guessed.

It was a large liner, an ideal place to hide. Did they have a cabin? In which case it would take hours to try and find them. He needed the Captain and all the crew on his side, but Rita and her friend were dangerous, only a small number of men could look for them and do so carefully not putting themselves in danger. he didn't want to waste time. He had a feeling they may not have a cabin in which case they, like the other passengers, would be on the decks watching the fading lights of Flåm.

He began his search. Would they keep to a large crowd, it was the best way of being unnoticed and, in effect, keeping hidden. He thought not. He had a sense that they would like to keep to themselves, find a place that was quieter from where they could keep a look out for anyone on their tail. They would not be on the decks from where everyone watched.

This particular cruise ship was not as large as some. He only had to head up one deck from where he'd boarded and he was on the same level as the lifeboats. There were fewer people here, but still, between the boats, some small groups were gathered.

He started on the port side walking slowly and casually from the stern towards the bow surreptitiously taking a look at each group or person he passed. There was no-one at the bow itself as people were more crowded to the stern and Flåm's lights.

He turned when he had gone as far as he could and began to go from bow to stern. He did not have to go far. He stopped. Just ahead of his were two people look back towards the stern and Flåm. One a woman, the other a man. Rita and her friend. The killer. Dag had to be careful, the man was surely armed. Ahead of them two large lifeboats were held by davits. Between them and Dag was a smaller craft, an inflatable tender used for quick transportation between the ship and shore. Dag ducked behind it and considered what to do.

His thoughts were broken into by the sound of an engine that rose above that of the ship's. Rita and Jan looked up at the same time as Dag. Its sound grew to cover that of the ship and abruptly lights burst overhead and the down-thrust of a helicopter washed over them.

At the very same moment a shout rang out. It came from ahead of him. A ship's officer stood by a door and had shouted at Rita and Jan.

"You two! May I have a word?"

He started towards them.

They both had their backs to the ships railing. Jan pulled out his weapon.

"No further!" he ordered. "Stand still!"

The officer stopped, wide eyed. Jørgen

"Now come here, slowly." Jan told him.

Dag could see the officer swallowed hard and didn't want to move.

"Move!" Jan shouted.

The officer moved.

Rita grabbed him by the arm. Jan's gun was pointed directly at his head. The officer looked terrified. Dag could just see their feet and the raised weapon from behind the tender. Rita and Jan had their backs to him. It was then he saw that Rita held a laptop under her left arm.

The ship gave a unexpected shudder. Dag stumbled forward onto the davit. The other three all felt the same movement. They too stumbled for a moment.

Rita's left arm had been leaning on the balustrade. It had also been holding the laptop. And she had not been holding it tightly enough or carefully enough. It slipped. Even from his position dag heard her gasp. Her right hand came away from the officer and reached out towards the laptop. It was too late. As if in slow motion Rita and Jan, as well as Dag, watched it turn and tumble towards the fjord. And all three pairs of eyes watched helplessly.

"What's going on?" a voice asked. Another crewman had appeared at the door way and was facing them.

Jan turned and re-pointed his weapon at the officer and now the crewman.

"Over here." He told the crewman. "Stand with your friend here."

He looked around at the tender. Dag ducked quickly out of sight.

"You two," Jan said waving his gun at the tender. "Get this thing launched. And don't say you can't. What else would you do in an emergency? Now move! Quickly. I won't hesitate to use this."

The two crewmen looked at each other.

"I mean it! Now! Move!" Jan said as he lifted the gun towards the officer's head. The officer nodded to the crewman and they turned to the tender.

Dag kept down and crawled away to get behind the cover of storage box.

"Stop!" Jan shouted. You! Don't move!"

Dag's luck had not held out. He'd been spotted. Slowly he got to his feet. He held his hands up.

"Turn round." Jan ordered.

Dag did as he was told. He saw the man holding the gun and could now see clearly that it was the one who'd got into the police station and stolen the memory stick.

"Well, well, Detective Inspector." Rita said using her most appealing voice. "I hadn't thought we'd meet so soon. Our plans were evidently not so well prepared as we thought."

Jan moved to the side and stood with bus back to the deck's wall so that he could keep them all under his gaze and his gun.

He spoke to the two crewmen. "You two, get that thing launched."

They hesitated. ""Do it now or one of you dies. And I don't care which one."

"Do as he says." Dag advised them.

They could still hear the sound of the helicopter's engine. It had been hovering over the fore deck. Now their throbbing and whine increased as it took off again.

The crew quickly set to work and in seconds they were ready to lower it.

"In you get." Jan told Rita. "And you," he said pointing the gun at the officer "you get in as well. I think we need some insurance. Go on get in."

The officer did as he was ordered first glancing at Dag who gave a slight nod.

"After all this you leave without the laptop." Dag said looking into Rita's eyes as she looked at him whilst climbing in to the tender.

"It is lost to both of us. That is, your friends in intelligence. At least they won't have it, not until they search the cold depths of this fjord and if anything useful remains on it."

"But why did you need it? You had the memory stick."

"We couldn't let your people have it now could we?"

The officer got into the tender under the aim of Jan's gun.

Dag had that feeling again. Her voice didn't sound right; it did have quite the same pitch as before. She was lying. Or, if not lying, it was not quite the truth.

Dag made a guess. "The memory stick; there was something wrong with it. You didn't get the data from it did you?" Perhaps, he thought, Ole Forsberg the computer hacker had done something to it.

Rita smiled. "If that were true then none of has now do we."

Jan climbed in to the tender his gun still carefully trained on the officer.

"Right," he said, "Lower us, and slowly, no funny business."

The crewman went to the lowering gear and asked Dag to help. The two of them under Jan's gaze began lowering the boat. The helicopter had taken off and was moving away up the valley.

"You won't get far" Dag called. "With a helicopter in the air they'll track you, hostage or not."

"We'll take that chance." Jan shouted back as the tender hit the water.

As soon as it did Jan ordered the officer to start the engine. As it roared in to life the door behind Dag and the crewman swung open and slammed the side of the wall. A figure burst through it and, almost before Dag had time to turn around; an arm and gun appeared beside him pointing at the now moving tender.

"No!" exclaimed Dag raising his hand. "They've got a hostage!"

He looked at the gun's owner, it was Rolf.

Martin and Rune jumped into Martin's car. It sped back through the tunnel to Flåm with Jørgen and Johan following close behind.

They headed to where Martin had dropped Dag off by the car park on the wharf-side. There were few cars there now as night had fallen and they parked up close to the water's edge. In the distance they could see the lights of the cruise ship as it headed towards the wider fjord to which this inlet was a final branch in the chain of valleys gouged by the ice age.

Martin and Rune walked to the water's edge as Jørgen and Johan parked up.

"You think he's on the ship?" Rune asked.

Martin nodded. "We were tricked, or at least you and I were, but not Dag. He had a feeling they slipped on to the ship."

They heard the sound of the helicopter's engine above that of the ship's. And, as the ship slowly edged around and disappeared behind a promontory, they saw the lights of the aircraft lifting from the ship. The ship itself seemed to slow down and stop, not quite disappearing as at first it had seemed. And its engines were louder.

"It's stopping." Rune said. "That's the sound of the engines in reverse."

The sound of another engine could just be heard. Rune shielded his eyes and looked out intensely into the darkness of the fjord.

"There's a small craft coming in to the harbour."

"From the ship?" asked Martin.

"I would think so."

"Us or them?"

"Them I suspect. They'll need to get to a position where they can disembark. And we need a position where we can wait for them; under cover. The buildings over there." Rune pointed to the buildings nearest the furthest point any boat to get to and they set off. Jørgen and Johan had stood behind them.

"You two can follow but keep well back and hidden." Martin told them.

Martin and Rune positioned themselves by the corner off a building with a good view of the harbour and still able to keep out of sight. The helicopter was circling over the fjord. A searchlight shone out from it down to the water's surface. It easily picked out the tender heading towards the harbour-side and descended to get closer. As it did so a shot rang out above the noise of its engines. The helicopter quickly ascended to a safer height some one hundred meters higher and circled in the air still trying to keep its searchlight on the boat.

Rune made phone call.

The tender was now almost half-way to the harbour.

The ship's crew were quick to ready a life boat for launch. The Captain was there to hasten them. They were well practiced and within minutes Dag and Rolf were clambering aboard along with two of the ship's crew, an officer and steersman. It swung out over the fjord and quickly descended to the water landing with a heavy jolt almost knocking them over. As soon as it hit the water the engines sprang to life and they were off in pursuit.

"So the laptop is under how much water and it seems the memory stick was compromised and no good to them. We did a bit of investigation on line, by the way. What's it all about?" Dag asked Rolf.

"Then you may have got an idea."

"Batteries." Dag said. "But that seemed innocent enough. Except, of course, there're reports on the internet about their military use, battlefield equipment and even underwater drones. And you happen to be Military Intelligence."

"Then you have an idea." Rolf said and paused. "Very well. Just between us. I shouldn't but learnt enough already. It's classified of course."

"Of course." Dag agreed.

"Just imagine a new generation of batteries, highly efficient, powerful, difficult to detect and running, to a great extent, off the simplest of materials. But, what if an agent, a sort of catalyst if you like, could be introduced during manufacture. Something that, given some specific circumstances, could result in the batteries failing."

Dag thought for a moment. "It would be pretty catastrophic for the military and their equipment. And they'd lose their underwater drones."

"Precisely."

"Thanks for telling me. I'll pretend I never heard it."

"It's best you forget."

The sound of a shot rang out over the fjord and the helicopter that had been keeping the tender under its spotlight veered away and rose in the air.

"Either a warning shot or an attempt to hit the searchlight." Rolf mused.

"We're not far from them."

"But they're gaining, they're faster than us."

"The chopper will keep them under surveillance won't it?"

"As far as possible. But once they're in the town they could escape us."

As he spoke his phone rang. He listened. "Stay in position," he replied, "and do what you think is necessary to stop them. But remember they have a hostage."

The call ended. "My man is in position." He told Dag. "And your detective is with him. They shouldn't get far."

"There's something I'd better tell you. A confession."

Rolf gave him a questioning stare.

"There's another copy of the memory stick. Purely by accident. We believe we copied it onto Martin's laptop."

"Really. I don't know whether to admonish you or thank you. And you have it I hope?"

"Dag nodded. "The girl at the hotel, the one who his Johan's laptop, hid mine as well."

"Then we'd best get our hand on it as quickly as possible. If those two know about it that's where they might be headed."

"I'm pretty sure that only knew about Johan's." Dag told him.

But he was wrong, Jan did know; he had watched Dag had it over from the cover of the trees.

Martin and Rolf waited. It was a still night and the tender moved fast across the still water. The minutes ticked away and as the tender came to the side of the harbour it was momentarily hidden. Then they saw Rita rise above it as she climbed some steps to the wharf-side. She paused and behind her came the ships officer, then followed by Jan keeping the man covered by his gun. Martin and Rune watched as the group looked carefully around. Satisfied it was all clear they started walking, Jan keeping close to the officer holding his arm and pointing the weapon to his side, keeping in front with Rita following.

They were coming almost directly to Martin and Rune's hiding place. There was nothing for it, thought Rune, but to come out and confront them.

Rune stepped out from the corner and took two quick places forward. Martin automatically followed him and stood to his side. Rune had already raised his weapon and from the corner of his eye all Martin could see was Rune's raised arm and the pistol.

"Halt or I fire!" Shouted Rune.

The three came to a halt.

Jan's arm moved upward to point his gun at the officer's head.

There was no warning.

The sound of the weapon being fired shattered the night's silence. Martin automatically jerked his head. The noise had almost deafened him. His eyes had shut at the same time. At virtually the same time a second shot rang out.

He opened them and looked. He could almost feel the heat of a gun's exhaust. It was Rune who had fired first. The second had been from Jan.

Rune's bullet had met its mark before Jan's finger had pulled the trigger. The force of the bullet hitting Jan had caused his arm and his hand to move. His arm had pulled forward pointing the gun just away from the officer's face. Just as his finger had automatically pulled on the trigger. The blast of the firing had almost brunt the officer's face and the bullet was expelled from the muzzle just a centimetre away from his nose.

Dag saw Jan. His eyes were, for a moment, open in surprise and shock. Then they closed. A patch of red spread out on his chest. His head sagged as did his legs. His knees gave way and he fell forward face down on the ground.

Behind where Jan had stood Rita now stood. She too looked surprised and then she looked shocked. She looked down at her chest. Martin saw a patch of red now growing on her chest. The bullet must have gone straight through Jan and into her.

The officer had raised his hands fearing that he might next.

Rune ran forwards.

"It's ok Sir, he told the officer, "You can put them down, you're safe now."

Rita was kneeling on the ground and Martin went over to her as Rune checked out Jan's body. Rune was already making a phone call.

Rita looked up at Martin. "You look a mess." She said with a faint smile.

"You don't look great yourself."

"It's not that bad. Jan took most of the force. The bullet hasn't gone far. I'll survive."

"Hmm, I wonder which prison cell."

"Oh, no prison cell for me. An arrangement will be made; eventually."

"Here," Martin said, bending down and handing her a handkerchief. "Press this on it; you don't want to lose too much blood."

"Thank you." She smiled. "Another time, who knows?"

Martin stood. The sound of sirens was already breaking the silence that seemed more intense after the sound of gunfire.

There was a commotion at the wharf-side. The lifeboat had arrived.

Dag and Rolf joined them. Two cars with blue flashing lights had appeared together with an ambulance. Dag could tell that the cars were not police vehicles.

Rolf commandeered one of the cars leaving Rune in charge of the 'clearing up' as he put it. Martin, Jørgen and Johan joined them and they set off to retrieve the laptop.

13.

They pulled up at the front of the hotel. Elise was on the reception desk.

"Still working?" Asked Dag.

"Yes," she sighed, "still working, it's been a long day; you just can't rely on staff these days."

Dag nodded agreement.

"Oh, Jørgen!" She said spotting him. "You're safe. That's wonderful!"

"We've come to see Ingrid. Is she about or do you know where she is?"

"Ingrid? Oh, well, now that's why I'm short staffed."

Dag frowned. "Where is she?" he asked again.

"You wouldn't believe it. Just packed her bags and left. Said she couldn't take any more. Just like that. Without a thank you. Not even asking for the money she was due. Just walked out."

"She's gone?" Jørgen said, surprised.

"When was this?" interrupted Dag.

""About a couple of hours ago."

"How did she leave? A taxi?"

"I don't think it was a taxi. But a car pulled up outside as soon as she went out of the door and picked her up."

"Describe the car." Rolf asked.

Elise thought. "It was dark I couldn't see that well. I can't be sure what colour but it was dark. And it was a large car. And I remember thinking; it was one of those like you see on the films with its windows blacked out."

"What was she carrying?" Dag asked her.

"Her suitcase."

"Anything else?"

Elise thought again. "She had something else in her other hand. It looked like a laptop, I think, yes a laptop I'm sure of it."

Dag looked at Rolf.

"Are you thinking what I'm thinking?"

"I think I am." Said Rolf as he got on his phone and made a call.

"Ingrid?" Martin asked Dag.

"Ingrid." Dag nodded.

Rolf finished his call.

"Well." Dag said to him. "I think we've done our bit. We've found our missing person, Johan here, and we've led you to Rita and Jan. I think that closes the case for us. I'll be happy to leave the rest to you. And best of luck."

Rolf nodded, held out his hand and shook Dag's. "I've a funny feeling I might need it. We never did find out what happened to the body, or who he really was."

"Oh," Dag added as Rolf turned away to leave, "you might want to have a word with Ole Forsberg, a computer hacker who gave us a bit of help. He lives in Kristiansund. I have a feeling that the memory stick Rita and Jan ended up with was not the one it should have been."

Rolf looked back. "Oh, thank you."

---------- * ----------

Characters

Dag Paulsen Meldel – Detective Inspector, Kristiansund Police
Martin Sorensen – Detective Sergeant, Kristiansund Police
Eduard Christiansen – Village Farmer
Petter Johansen – Murdered man's assumed name
Bjorn Hagen - Forensics team leader
Aksel Hansen – Village Local Boy
Johan Christiansen – Eduard's nephew
Kevin Vikan – Chemical plant manager
Andreas Østrem – Police computer expert
Ole Forsberg – Computer hacker
Markus Dagestad - Johan Christiansen' pseudonym
Jenny Strøm – Detective Constable, Kristiansund Police
Rolf - E-tjenesten Agent 1- E14
Roar - E-tjenesten Agent 2- E14
Håkon Eriksen –Chief Inspector, Kristiansund Police
Jan Haaland/Vaižgantas Svilas/Patrik Sandberg –Agent
Jørgen Arnesen – Johan's second cousin
Elise – Manageress of Flåm Hotel
Ingrid – Receptionist at Flåm Hotel
Eirik – Sous Chef at Flåm Hotel
Sigurd Eriksen – Barman at the Cockerel Microbrewery
Sven – barman at the Cockerel Microbrewery
Theo Osen – Sigurd's uncle, owner of the Cockerel Microbrewery
Rita Hustad – Agent
Rune - E-tjenesten Agent 3 - E14

Printed in Great Britain
by Amazon